Pull this cracker to dis[c]
a spooky carol-singing

...he cracker without careful inspection by
...ist Pat Thomson. All the stories are tried
and tested favourites for sharing with young children, and by top
children's authors – Robert Swindells, Richmal Crompton,
Marjorie Darke, Alison Uttley and many others.

PAT THOMSON is a well-known author and anthologist.
Additionally, she works as a lecturer and librarian in a teacher
training college – work which involves a constant search for short
stories which have both quality and child-appeal. She is also an
Honorary Vice-President of the Federation of Children's Book
Groups. She is married with two grown-up children and lives in
Northamptonshire.

'05

Also available by Pat Thomson,
and published by Corgi Books:

A BUS FULL OF STORIES FOR FOUR YEAR OLDS

A POCKETFUL OF STORIES FOR FIVE YEAR OLDS

A BUCKETFUL OF STORIES FOR SIX YEAR OLDS

A BASKET OF STORIES FOR SEVEN YEAR OLDS

A SACKFUL OF STORIES FOR EIGHT YEAR OLDS

A CHEST OF STORIES FOR NINE YEAR OLDS

A SATCHEL OF SCHOOL STORIES

A STOCKING FULL OF CHRISTMAS STORIES

A CRACKER full of Christmas Stories

Collected by
PAT THOMSON

Illustrated by Jon Riley

CORGI BOOKS

A CRACKER FULL OF CHRISTMAS STORIES

A CORGI BOOK : 0 552 52805 6

First published in Great Britain by Doubleday,
a division of Transworld Publishers Ltd

PRINTING HISTORY
Doubleday edition published 1994
Corgi edition published 1995

Corgi Books are published by Transworld Publishers Ltd,
61–63 Uxbridge Road, Ealing, London W5 5SA,
in Australia by Transworld Publishers (Australia) Pty Ltd,
15–25 Helles Avenue, Moorebank, NSW 2170,
and in New Zealand by Transworld Publishers (NZ) Ltd,
3 William Pickering Drive, Albany, Auckland.

Printed and bound in Great Britain by
Cox & Wyman Ltd, Reading, Berkshire

Acknowledgements

The editor and publisher are grateful for permission to include the following copyright stories:

Richmal Crompton, 'The Christmas Truce' from *William's Happy Days*. Reprinted by permission of Macmillan Publishers Ltd.

Marjorie Darke, 'Christmas Crackers' © Marjorie Darke 1983, from *Mists and Magic* selected and edited by Dorothy Edwards. Reprinted by permission of Rogers, Coleridge & White Ltd.

Rumer Godden, 'Loving and Giving' © Rumer Godden 1973 from *The Noel Streatfeild Summer Holiday Book*. Reprinted by permission of Curtis Brown on behalf of Rumer Godden.

Grace Hallworth, 'Images in Bethlehem' © Grace Hallworth 1990, from *A Web of Stories*. Reprinted by permission of Methuen Children's Books.

George Layton, 'The Christmas Party' from *A NORTHERN CHILD-HOOD: The Balaclava Boys and Other Stories* published by Longman Group UK Ltd.

C. G. Leland, 'The Twelfth-Night King' from *A Noble Company* ed C. G. Compton, first published 1931.

George Mackay Brown, 'The Lost Boy' from *Andrina and Other Stories* published by The Hogarth Press. Reprinted by permission of Random Century Ltd.

Janet McNeill, 'The Small Brown Mouse' from *A Light Dozen* by Janet McNeill. Reprinted by permission of A. P. Watt Ltd on behalf of Janet Alexander.

Maurice and Pamela Michael, 'The Christmas Present' from *German Fairy Tales* published by Frederick Muller Ltd, first published 1958.

Ruth Sawyer, 'The Christmas Apple' from *The Lost Half Hour* published by The Bodley Head.

CONTENTS

A CRACKER FULL OF
CHRISTMAS STORIES

Christmas Crackers

I like Christmas. Usually it's great, but this year nothing went right. Mum had flu, we forgot to put the Christmas pud on in time, Lucy made lumpy custard and Budge emptied the lot over his high chair. The turkey was OK though. Me and Dad cooked that. All the same, Christmas dinner didn't taste right with Mum in bed. After, we kept arguing about which telly programmes to watch – in whispers because Mum's head was splitting. By tea-time everyone felt Christmas was a wash-out.

'Biscuits in the blue tin, Luce,' Dad said brightly. 'Box of crackers in the sideboard, Steve,' and to Budge: 'Come and help me get the cake.'

We knew he was trying to cheer us up, but joining in was difficult. Budge didn't try. He just sucked his thumb. But, then, he's only a baby.

We had tea on the floor. None of us could be bothered to set the table. Just as well because Lucy fell over pulling her cracker, which made everyone laugh and feel a bit better. Inside the crackers were paper hats and presents and riddles.

Lucy pushed her crown out of her eyes to read: '*What can go up a chimney down, but not down a chimney up?*'

I'd seen that in a comic. 'Umbrella.'

She snorted like she does when anyone gets the better of her. 'Go on, then, Bighead, read yours.'

'It's a daft poem,' I said. '*Wind whistle – Gale blow – Spell my name – Then I'll know.* Know what?'

'The answer, silly.'

'All right, Clever, what's the answer then?'

'I didn't say I *knew*, I only said what the riddle *meant*.'

'Same thing,' I pointed out.

'The answers are on the back,' Dad said in a shut-up-Steve voice.

I looked. 'Just my Christmas luck. They've

2

forgotten to print it! What am I supposed to do
. . . spell S.P.E.L.L.?'

'Stop moaning.' Lucy held out a little plastic
black cat charm. 'Your whistle's better than this.
At least it makes a noise. Blow!'

I blew, but the only sound was the phone
ringing. Dad had Budge on his knee, playing a
game with him and his little cracker dinosaur toy,
so I got up to answer.

'Is that you, Stephen?' asked a man's voice.

'Yes.'

'Good, good. Phoning to let you know I'm
catching the one-fifteen flight. Touch-down at
two.'

My brain felt full of Christmas stodge. 'Touch-
down?'

The voice said: 'Yes, touch-down. You know
. . . Arrival!' in a brisk sort of way, as if I was
being thick.

'Who's speaking?' I asked.

'Ernest, of course. See you near two. I'd like
to be more precise, but when Martha pilots there's
no knowing! Oh . . . give my love to Lucy.'
There was a click and the line went dead before
I could ask did he mean Boxing Day afternoon
and what airport and who was Martha?

'Wrong number,' Dad said after I'd told him.

3

'We don't know any Ernests or Marthas,' and he began reading us a Brer Rabbit story, doing crazy voices till we fell about laughing.

After that it was bed-time.

I woke in the dark with Lucy shaking my shoulder. 'Steve . . . wake up, can't you! Steve!'

I tried to get back into this great dream I was having about a cream doughnut, and buried my head under the pillow.

She dragged the pillow away. 'Steve, there's a man on the balcony.'

'Burglartelldad . . .'

'STEVE!' Yanking off the bedclothes she gave me such a shove I nearly fell on to the floor.

I shouted: 'Lemmealone!'

But she just grabbed my pyjama jacket and began tugging me towards the hall. 'He's got a bowler hat, and an umbrella that he keeps knocking on the window with, and he's pulling faces at Budge'n me.'

Lucy and Budge share the bedroom that looks out on to the balcony.

'Burglars don't knock,' I said. And only then did it hit me that there's no way on to that balcony except *through* their bedroom – our flat being eight floors up in the tower block, and the fire-escape on the kitchen side.

Lucy had left the door open and as we got to it our eyes nearly fell out with surprise. Running round Budge's cot rail like a live mouse was the dinosaur he'd got out of his cracker. *Nobody making it work!* Budge, standing up clutching the rail, was giggling like mad every time the thing scampered over his fingers. Watching from the other side of the cot was this tall thin man in a pin-striped suit and bowler, holding an umbrella.

He smiled at us. 'Hallo! Budge said to come in. Hope you don't mind . . . as you two sent the messages,' he added, and hooked his umbrella handle over a moonbeam shining between the curtains. With a flick of his wrist he sent the silver light sliding on to the umbrella spike and wrote:

'STEVE LUCY BUDGE
HAPPY CHRISTMAS'

in the air, just as if it was a Biro. The letters hung glittering like sparklers.

I hadn't a clue what he was talking about and Lucy looked blank. I mean – Budge can't talk that much. And what messages? Who was this weirdie anyway?

As if he'd tuned into my brain, he clicked his tongue, tapping a finger on my forehead. Somehow, when he took his hand away, he was holding a pad with DON'T FORGET printed in red across the top. There was a pencil dangling from it on a string.

'Ernest's the name. I told you before. Write it down.'

'Cor!' Lucy breathed, as I took the pad and tried but couldn't make the letters work. 'He pulled it straight out of your head like a drawer. How did you do it, Ernest?'

Ernest's smile grew bigger. 'Like this!' pulling a long gold streamer from Budge's ear and tossing it high so it looped round the sparkly letters.

'Or this.' He put a hand between my neck and pyjama collar, bringing out two of the biggest cream doughnuts in the world. He gave us one each. Then leaned over the cot, taking a chocolate rabbit from Budge's bare toe.

Lucy's eyes got wider and wider. Ernest looked smug.

'How about this then?' He snapped his fingers.

It was as if someone had taken the weights off Lucy's feet. She floated up into the air, spread her arms and sailed round the room. Ernest looked at me.

'Want a go?'

I nodded.

He nodded . . . and there I was zooming past the picture rail, over the wardrobe, circling the light bulb, then swooping close to Budge's head as he sucked his rabbit and stared. It was smashing! Finally we landed.

'Oh Ernest, you *are* clever,' Lucy gasped.

'It's nothing,' he said modestly, but anyone could see he was chuffed to blazes. He drew a clock face on the floor and looked at the hands. 'Time's nearly up . . . but perhaps we've enough minutes left for one more trick. What'll it be?' and before anyone said anything: 'Right you are, Lucy!' pointing his umbrella at her dressing-gown pocket which began to bulge and wriggle. A black furry head popped up. Two big green eyes looked at us, then round the room. Before you could blink, a streak of black whizzed through the air and landed on the cot rail, missing the dinosaur by a hair. It fell upside down in Budge's cot. The kitten followed. There were hisses and squeaks, then howls from Budge.

Lucy yelled: 'It'll eat it!' She dashed for the cot, on the way accidentally hooking an arm through a streamer loop, then tripping up. I heard a tinkling crash like windows breaking, and saw the letters fall in a shattered heap. Budge howled louder still, and in the middle of the racket Dad appeared in the doorway, steamed up and ready to tell us off. But the words never happened. What did happen was Ernest whirling his umbrella, shouting:

'STOP!'

And we did. Like a film breaking down. Only Ernest could move. He drew back the curtains. Outside, hovering over our balcony, was a shadow. It was shaped like a garden broom, with an old-fashioned plane cockpit at the handle end, and inside it – I'm not sure, but it might've been a pointed hat.

'She's on time. Splendid!' Ernest said, and using his umbrella, did a neat pole vault, slotting himself feet first through the open window, like an envelope through a letter-box. I saw him disappear into the cockpit. Two hands waved. A fading voice called:

'GOOD . . . by . . . e . . .'

The moon went behind a cloud.

Sometimes when you wake up in bed in the mornings there are dream bits hanging about in your head. Nothing makes sense. It was like that, Boxing Day morning.

Lucy came into my room hugging a black kitten. 'Look what Mum's given me!'

I sat up. '*Mum?*'

She frowned, sort of puzzled. 'I . . . think . . . so.'

On the chair of my bed was an empty DON'T FORGET pad. A pencil too – on a string. I picked them up.

'*Wish* I knew,' I muttered.

'What?'

But I was watching sprawly purple letters writing themselves across the pad:

> *Wish right,*
> *Wish well,*
> *Yours ever,*
> *Ernest Spell.*

Lucy peered over my shoulder just as I was working out my second wish. 'Who's Ernest Spell?'

Quickly I stuffed the pad under my pillow. If she didn't know, I wasn't going to tell her.

From the kitchen Mum called to us: 'Breakfast. Move, you two! Dad's getting our bikes out. We've got a lot to do today.'

They'd worked! Both wishes had really

10

worked. Good old Ernest. Now if we were going for a bike ride and someone had a puncture . . .

I grinned at Lucy. 'Tell you later,' I said and started pulling on my jeans.

This story is by Marjorie Darke.

The Christmas Present

Once upon a time there lived a stocking-weaver, called Paul Nicholas, with his wife and six children. There were three boys and three girls. The boys had dark hair and light eyes, like their mother, and the girls had chestnut hair and deep blue eyes, like their father. They were a very happy family because they all loved one another and helped each other, but there was not always enough work for the weaver and they were very, very poor. Sometimes they even went short of food and they were never able to have nice clothes or toys, like the children of richer parents. However, they were never envious or sad, and they certainly never complained. Each one of the family did his or her best to help to make life easier for the others. The girls helped their mother in the house, and the boys went off into the forest to collect firewood. In the summer and autumn they would all go out and pick mushrooms and nuts and blackberries which they sold in the town. The boys also did odd jobs for some of the farmers in the neighbourhood, which earned them a little money and helped buy food for the rest of the family.

Winter was the worst time of all the year for the weaver and his family, everything cost more money and work was scarcer to find. One winter, just before Christmas, the weaver had set his heart on giving some little treat to his wife and children at a time when everyone should be merry and glad. He had worked extra hard at his loom, trudged many long journeys into the towns to try to sell his stockings, but he met with little success. He scarcely earned enough money to keep his poor family from starving, let alone to give them presents or treats. He could not bear to think of them having to watch the beautiful Christmas trees being carried into their neighbours' houses, and to see the sparkling trinkets and toys in the shop windows, knowing that there would be none in their home that Christmas Eve.

The children would see others making merry and feasting all around, while they might even have to go hungry. Paul knew that they would not grumble, but his eyes filled with tears when he realized that he could do so little for his good, uncomplaining family.

Perhaps you can imagine his relief and joy when, just two weeks before Christmas, he was given an order by a merchant for as many stockings as he could weave by Christmas Eve. He hurried home with the good news, and how happy and excited the children all were, when he told them about his stroke of good fortune and how it meant that he would have enough money to give them a delicious Christmas dinner and a Christmas tree hung with presents for them all. They jumped and shouted and laughed, for never had they known the promise of so many good things, and that just when their luck seemed to be most against them. For the next week or more Paul hardly ate or slept he worked so hard and such long hours, so as to have a huge sackful of stockings to take to the merchant in the town. When the time came for him to set out, he told the boys to fetch a big fir branch from the forest for their Christmas tree and he promised that he

would bring back presents for them all and a goose for their Christmas dinner. They all stood at the door of the cottage and watched him trudge off down the lane with the bulging sack thrown over his shoulder.

It was a lovely winter's day. Thick, crisp snow on the ground and a frosty clear blue sky above, from which the sun shone down on the weaver as he swung along, so happy at the thought of the treats in store for his family that he forgot his sack was heavy and the road long, and he never felt tired at all. He only stopped once at a farm where he saw a fine fat goose in the yard and asked the farmer how much money he wanted for it. The farmer could see that Paul was a poor man, and as he was in a kindly, Christmassy mood he said he would let him have it very cheap. The weaver explained that he would have plenty of money to pay for it on his way back from town and that he would collect it then to take home for his family's Christmas dinner. 'Won't they have a feast!' he smiled to himself as he walked on towards the town faster than ever.

When he reached the town, he went straight to the merchant's house, but there he found to his grief and horror, that the merchant was not at home. He had gone away only an hour earlier and his clerk told Paul that he must come back for his money three days later, when the merchant would have returned home.

The poor weaver was numb with dismay. He begged the clerk for a small part of the money that was owing to him so that at least he could buy some bread for his hungry children, but the clerk said he had no money with which to pay him and that he must just wait three days. 'Where has your master gone?' asked Paul, 'perhaps if I hurry I may overtake him?' The clerk replied that his master had ridden away on his fastest horse and that no-one could possibly catch him up on foot.

Then, indeed, the weaver's heart sank, and he realized he could gain nothing by asking any more questions. He took up his empty sack and turned his face homewards. How the day had changed! The morning that had been so sunny and bright had given way to a gloomy late afternoon. Clouds had covered the sun, and the sky, that had been so sparkling and blue, was like lead. As dull and heavy as the poor weaver's heart. At last, he began to realize how tired he was, and he plodded along thinking of the eager faces waiting for him at home and wondering how he was ever going to break the news to them and see their disappointment, when they realized that instead of a feast and nice presents, they were to go to bed without any supper and without one little toy to hang on their bare Christmas tree.

His mind was so filled with these sad thoughts that he never noticed how late it was and how dark it had grown in the forest, until suddenly his attention was caught by some bright little lights shining through the trees. Greatly surprised at this strange sight he left the path and walked towards the lights until he came to a clearing round which dozens of shining little lanterns were hung from the branches of the trees, as well as hundreds of apples and pears and nuts and sweets and toys. As Paul stood there, with his mouth hanging open with astonishment, a little gentleman – quite the smallest little gentleman he had ever seen – came up to him. He was most beautifully and elegantly dressed in expensive furs, with red leather boots and a cap made from the skin of a white mouse! He was no more than a foot high and so very unusual that the weaver did not know whether to laugh or to be afraid.

The tiny man bowed politely and said 'You are Paul, the weaver, and we know that you are hungry and tired and sad, because you have nothing to take home to your wife and children

for Christmas – and very nice children they are too, *particularly* the young ladies!' The weaver had never heard his little girls called young ladies before, so he took off his hat to the small gentleman and thanked him for the compliment.

'Now,' said the little man, 'you must have some refreshment, for you will need all your strength for the journey home, as that sack of yours is going to be full and heavy.' He led Paul to a little shelter made of tree bark and fir branches where a small fire burnt brightly and a small table was laid with a snowy white cloth and beside it stood a chair made from a tree root. On the table was a bottle of wine and a covered plate from which came the most perfectly delicious smell. The little man nodded to the table and said to Paul: 'Eat!' Greatly wondering, the weaver sat down and uncovered the dish. He needed no more encouragement, for although he had no idea of what the dish was made – except that it had a strong flavour of hare and mushrooms and rich brown gravy – he knew that he had never tasted anything so wonderfully delicious in all his life.

'Drink!' said the little man, pointing to the bottle, and Paul poured out a glass of sparkling ruby-red wine for himself and raised it to his lips. He was just about to drink when he paused to ask, 'Please tell me your name, kind sir, so that I may drink to your health?' 'Drink to your family at home first,' replied the little man, 'and then I will tell you my name.'

Paul gladly drank to his wife and their six children. 'And now you may drink to me,' said the strange little man with a grave smile. 'My name is Count Charles Goodfriend.'

The weaver drank the Count's health and felt the good red wine warm and cheer him, then he rose to his feet, wished the little man a merry Christmas and thanked him most gratefully for all his kindness and hospitality.

'Wait, wait a moment,' said the little Count, 'do you think you could manage to carry something in that sack of yours?' The weaver thought that he could, and the Count led the way to the trees which were hung with so many good things. 'Take as many of these as your sack will hold,' said the little Count, 'but if you will let me give you some advice, I should take mostly apples and pears.' The weaver did as he was asked and not wishing to seem too greedy or to disobey the Count's request he did take more apples and pears than any of the other things, though he also found room for a good many sweets and toys as well. When his sack was stuffed full he hoisted it on to his back with many words of thanks to the kind little man, and just as he was leaving Count Goodfriend spoke a few more words of advice to him.

'Take care of what you have got and make good use of it, for it is a reward to you and your wife and children for being kind to one another and to other people, and for not complaining about your hard lives.'

As the little man stopped speaking the lights among the trees suddenly faded and went out, and the weaver found himself alone in the darkness. If it had not been for the full and heavy sack on his back he might have wondered if the whole thing had not been a dream. He found his way back to the road and set off towards home briskly and happily. He was so pleased at having so many nice things for the children that he didn't mind the weight on his back, although in some strange way it seemed to grow heavier with every step. But as he reached the outskirts of his village, the sack had really grown so enormously heavy that he had to set it down and ask a passer-by to help him carry it. After a little while the sack had become even heavier and was too much for the two of them, so that they asked another passer-by to help them. A little further still and the three of them could scarcely stagger along with this enormous load and they were obliged to ask a fourth person to help them carry it. At last the four men, panting and struggling reached the weaver's house and dumped the sack down by the door. Paul thanked his helpers warmly and they all went off wishing each other a merry Christmas. The children and their mother were gazing out of the window, their eyes round with astonishment and they all came rushing out to Paul to ask however many good things he had brought in his sack that had needed four men to carry it. The weaver called out merrily, 'Come along and have a look for yourselves – there are nuts and sweets and apples and pears and toys and cakes—' The children opened up the sack and nuts, cakes, sweets and toys were there, but wonder of wonders – all the apples and pears had turned into gold and silver money!

They were all speechless with amazement, then they all laughed and shouted as they saw the great glittering pile of money.

The weaver told his family all about this strange meeting with Count Goodfriend, and he did not forget to say what the little man had told him about making good use of his present. 'If we want our good luck to continue and this treasure to bring us the blessings of happiness as well as wealth, then the first thing we must do is to find someone less fortunate than ourselves and bring them some happiness too.' The children were delighted to think of helping other people, and they found twenty poor children who would have gone dinnerless and gave them a feast on Christmas Day that they remembered all their lives.

Paul, the weaver, continued to use his fairy-given fortune so kindly and so wisely that he became first a famous stocking-weaver, then a rich merchant and finally the mayor of his town. In spite of his high position he never ceased to help and think of those people who had less than himself. He and his wife and their children and grandchildren were always kind and loving to each other, and eager to help any poor honest people who had not been lucky enough to make the acquaintance of Count Charles Goodfriend.

This story is by Maurice and Pamela Michael.

Images in Bethlehem

They came to Bethlehem at dusk
A man, a woman on an ass
Gently he lifted her from its back
She swayed unsteady on her feet
    and clung to him
For a moment they stood
Three figures etched against the canvas of a
    darkening sky like silhouettes.

I came out of the inn and saw the travellers near the well.

'Shalom!' the man greeted me. 'Good friend, will you stay with Mary my wife, while I speak with the inn-keeper?'

'Master,' I said, 'if you seek lodging you will not find any here. Even on the cold floor of the cook-house travellers spread their sleeping mats at night.'

But the man would not be put off.

'I must try for my wife's sake,' he said. 'She is weak from the journey and needs rest.'

And he hurried into the inn.

Mary's eyes were gentle and wise beyond her years. I think that she was not much older than my thirteen years. The man could have been father to her. I sat down beside her on the resting stone.

'I am Naomi and work here at the inn. Have you journeyed far?'

'Five days we have been on the road from Nazareth. After the second day of our journey, Joseph's mule was stolen and he is weary and footsore, though he tries to hide it from me.'

'Have you no friends in Bethlehem where you might find shelter?' I asked.

'Oh yes,' she answered, 'we shall stay with Joseph's family in the city but we need a place to rest tonight.'

We saw Joseph coming and rose to meet him.

'Mary, my beloved, we must go on to the next inn. There is no room here,' he said.

'The next inn!' I exclaimed. I looked at the three travellers. The man's eyes were red-rimmed from lack of sleep, the woman was big with child, and the donkey! Well, they would be robbed, or worse, just for that bag of bones of a donkey. They wouldn't get as far as the next village and that was closer than the next inn. I made up my mind.

'Come with me,' I said. 'I have a shelter close by. There you'll be safe and warm for the night.'

My lantern's thin beam of light pointed the way through pine forest and up a rough narrow track. On either side there were steep rock walls honeycombed with caves. My cave was the last and well-hid. Even in the light of day you could pass the entrance and not see it. The cave was dark and cold when we entered. Maybe it would seem frightening to a stranger but since my mother had died and left me an orphan, it was home to me. I knew every step of ground and patch of wall in it. I kindled a fire and soon the cave was warm and bright. The animals – a cow and its calf, a ram and two ewes – had settled down for the night but when the donkey ambled across to join them they made room for it.

'Are these your animals?' asked Joseph.

'No,' I said, 'when I found the cave they were already here. We share in peace.'

We supped well on a loaf of bread and chunks of fish baked with olives I had brought with me from the inn. Afterwards we drank fresh goat's milk and ate some dates. I offered them my bed made with pine branches and hay. Every week I changed the hay so the bed was sweet and clean.

'Where will *you* sleep?' Mary asked.

'I will be warm enough near the animals. I often sleep with them when the nights are cold,' I said. And that was the truth.

She hugged and kissed me. Joseph put his hands on my head and said, 'Peace be with you always, Naomi. You have fed and sheltered, and even given your bed to strangers.'

He took some bedding from a bundle and laid a blanket over the branches and hay for Mary to lie on. He spread another over her to keep her warm. Then he laid himself down on his sleeping mat.

Soon there was only the sound of crackling as the firewood burned.

There was peace in the cave.

The hills of Bethlehem resound
with rhapsodies from distant spheres
a paean of peace and joy
And hosts of angels from on high
swirling and whirling like dervishes
in a dance of ecstasy
worship a baby boy.

Next morning I said to Joseph, 'Master, I can see that Mary will soon give birth. Rest here awhile for her sake.'

It was well that he agreed for on that very night the child was born. And what a night it was!

When the animals heard the baby crying they crowded around.

At once the child began to make happy sounds as though he was laughing and talking with the animals. Then they knelt down before the baby and made *their* noises. To hear them you would have thought they were trying to sing a lullaby.

In the midst of all this we heard a scuffling sound outside the cave and a man entered carrying a lamb. When he saw us he drew back and said, 'I didn't know that anyone lived here. My flock grazes on the meadows beyond the hills above. I heard the cries of animals and came to see whether any of mine had strayed.'

I welcomed him and showed him the animals kneeling around the baby.

'Glory be! What kind of child is this that animals kneel before him?' he asked in wonder.

'You come in time to celebrate our son's birth,' said Joseph. 'Will you share some mead with us?'

'Gladly,' said the shepherd, 'and offer as a gift my lamb who followed me of her own accord.'

Suddenly the animals ceased their cries.

There was a great stillness.

The fire I had lit earlier was dying but the cave was flooded with a light so bright that there was not a dark place or shadow in it. As I looked around I saw that each face shone as though it was lit up from inside, and the baby was bathed in a golden glow. All the lines of pain had gone from around Mary's eyes and they were soft with love.

The shepherd broke the silence.

'Strange! I came here weary and cold from tramping the hills. Now, I want to run and leap and shout for joy. What has happened? I have never felt like this.'

'The mead was strong and makes us merry and light of spirit,' I said. Yet even as I said it I knew that was not the reason. And Mary smiled as

32

though she held a secret too precious to share with us.

'What will you call your son?'

'His name is Jeshua,' said Mary.

'A name that is rightly his,' said the shepherd, 'for I believe that he is the One who will bring salvation to his people, as it has been foretold by the prophets.'

And everyone present was filled with joy that night, and marvelled.

> To Bethlehem the Magi came
> following a bright new star.
> It hung o'er hillside bleak and bare
>   an iridescent pearl
>   guiding true seekers on the way
> to a lowly stall whereon the Christ child lay
>   in perfect bliss.

It was just seven days after the birth of Jeshua that three strangers came to the inn. I could see from their clothes and manner that they were important men, and wealthy too with all their following of servants.

They said that they were seeking a baby. This was no ordinary child but a great king and saviour. They offered a reward to anyone who knew of a

baby born within the month. I was sure that they were looking for Mary's baby. I had not told anyone at the inn about the birth, so when the men left I followed them and told them all that had happened on the night that Jeshua was born. They got very excited and asked me to lead them to the cave.

When they entered the cave the men greeted Mary and Joseph as though they were great people and knelt before the baby, just as the animals did on the night of his birth.

'We have travelled through many lands to find this child who is destined for greatness,' said one who appeared to be the eldest.

'Master, they say that the strange light we saw in the cave came from a special star that appears when a great king is born,' I said.

'My wife has been forewarned that the child will be a true rabbi of Jehovah,' said Joseph. 'But now you talk about a great king!'

'Josephus, we cannot tell you why or how these things will come to pass, for even the wisest of us is but a fool in the presence of the great power that rules the universe.'

They all believed in the movements of the planets and were able to predict events according to these movements. Each had seen the special star and knew what it meant so they had set out on a quest. They brought with them gifts for the baby. There were casks of polished wood which held sweet-smelling perfumes, myrrh and frankincense, and a casket in which there was a crown of gold set with diamonds and precious stones.

We were tongue-tied at the sight of such wonderful gifts. Then Mary spoke and there was something in her voice I had not heard before. A sort of pride.

'Wise and noble lords who have journeyed so far to pay homage to our son,' she said, 'we rejoice at the tidings you bring and are honoured by these gifts so costly and so rare. All that has happened here we will guard in our hearts and reveal to Jeshua when he is old enough to understand.'

Before they left the men drew Master and myself aside and said, 'King Herod asked us to let him know as soon as we found the child but we have been disturbed by dreams and omens. We believe that he intends harm to the child. You must leave this place as soon as you can. And you, Naomi, must tell no-one where the child is.'

The Master believed the men because they seemed so wise, and he feared for his son's life but Mary never doubted that what had been prophesied would be fulfilled.

Early the following morning Master said, 'Naomi, today I shall go to the city to visit my family so that they may prepare a place of safety for us.'

I was uneasy about leaving Mary and the baby alone so I said, 'I will stay here while you are

36

gone. When you leave cover the entrance with branches from the myrtle tree so that it is hidden.'

Master never got to the city.

He told us that on his way there he saw soldiers pursuing mothers who were trying to find hiding places for their babies. He said that when he saw the mangled bodies of babies lying in his path he turned around and started back to the cave.

Meanwhile, Mary and I did not know what was happening outside until we heard the tramp of boots and shouting of men's voices. I knew at once that they were soldiers searching the caves. There was no telling what they might find in some of them for it was rumoured that robbers and murderers used the caves as a hide-out.

I showed Mary a niche at the back of our cave where she could hide the child and we hid all signs of a baby's presence. Mary sat quietly whilst I went to the entrance to listen for sounds of footsteps coming our way.

There were just two of them.

'Let us look closely. There may be something behind the branches,' said one soldier.

'How could anyone get past such a web and not disturb it?' asked the other. 'Look at the layers of webbing, man! That must have taken many days to spin. What a beauty!'

This soldier seemed more interested in the spider's web than looking for a baby.

'But if there was more than one spider the web could have been made in a few hours,' persisted the first soldier.

'Nay, there is but one weaver. A lone spider and there he is,' said the other. 'Besides there is a sign here that means danger. Let it be.'

I heard them walking away but did not breathe until their footsteps faded. Mary and I wondered though, what he meant by a sign of danger, but we dared not go out of the cave in case other soldiers were about.

It seemed a long time after that the Master returned. He came in quietly and was as pale as the waning moon.

He said he would never forget the faces of the dead children, the sound of mothers weeping and the fathers' curses as they watched the slaughter of their innocent children.

Nor would he forget what he saw outside the cave when he returned. He described the enormous web a spider had woven that morning. A web that covered the branches he had placed in front of the entrance and the area all around it. And most amazing of all, was the sign of a cross beneath the webbing! A sign which meant danger for the soldiers but salvation for Jeshua and his parents.

A tiny spider, one of the smallest of creatures, helped to save the life of the Christ child.

The inn is packed at this time of year. Now that it belongs to me I turn no-one away who wishes to stay. And each year on the night of Jeshua's birth I tell the story to those who are here. And strange to say, each year on this night, a spider spins a web over the door of the cave.

This story is by Grace Hallworth.

The Christmas Party

Our classroom looked smashing. Lots of silver
tinsel and crepe paper and lanterns. *We'd* made
the lanterns, but Miss Taylor had bought the rest
herself, out of her own money. Oh, only today
and tomorrow and then we break up. Mind you,
if school was like this all the time, I wouldn't be
bothered about breaking up. Putting up Christmas decorations and playing games – much
better than doing writing and spelling any day. I
watched the snow coming down outside. Smashing! More sliding tomorrow. I love Christmas. I
wish it was more than once a year. Miss Taylor
started tapping on the blackboard with a piece of

chalk. Everybody was talking and she kept on tapping until the only person you could hear was Norbert Lightowler.

'Look if I get a six and land on you, you get knocked off and I still get another go!'

The whole class was looking at him.

'Look, when Colin got a six, he landed on *me* and *he* got another . . . !'

Suddenly he realized that he was the only one talking and he started going red.

'Thank you, Norbert, I think we all know the rules of Ludo.'

Miss Taylor can be right sarcastic sometimes. Everybody laughed. Even Miss Taylor smiled.

'Now, since it is getting so noisy, we're going to stop these games and do some work.'

Everybody groaned and Tony and me booed – quietly so Miss Taylor couldn't hear. She hates people that boo. She says people who boo are cowards.

'Who is that booing?'

We must have been booing louder than we thought.

'Who is that booing?'

Miss Taylor looked at Tony. I looked at Tony. They both looked at me. I put my hand up.

'It was me, Miss.'

Tony put his hand up.

'It was me an' all, Miss.'

She looked at us.

'You both know what I think of booing, don't you?'

We nodded.

'Yes, Miss.'

'Yes, Miss.'

'Don't ever let me hear it again.'

We shook our heads.'

'No, Miss.'

'No, Miss.'

She turned to the class.

'Now, the work I have in mind is discussion work.'

Everybody groaned again, except me and Tony.

'I thought we'd discuss tomorrow's Christmas party!'

We all cheered and Miss Taylor smiled. We have a Christmas party every year, the whole school together in the main hall. Each class has its own table and we all bring the food from home.

'Now, does everybody know what they're bringing from home for the party tomorrow?'

I knew. I was bringing a jelly. I put my hand up.

'I'm bringing a jelly, Miss!'

Everybody started shouting at once and Miss Taylor moved her hands about to calm us down.

'All right, all right, one at a time. Don't get excited. Jennifer Greenwood, what are you bringing?'

Jennifer Greenwood was sitting in the back row next to Valerie Burns. She wriggled her shoulders and rolled her head about and looked down. She always does that when she's asked a question. She's daft is Jennifer Greenwood.

'C'mon, Jennifer, what are you bringing for tomorrow?'

She put her hand up.

'Please, Miss, I'm bringing a custard trifle, Miss.'

Norbert Lightowler pulled his mouth into a funny shape and pretended to be sick.

'Ugh, I hate custard. I'm not gonna have any of that!'

Everybody laughed, except Miss Taylor.

'Well, Norbert, if I was Jennifer I wouldn't dream of giving you any. Right, Jennifer?'

Jennifer just rolled her head about and giggled with Valerie Burns. Norbert was looking down at his desk.

'And, Norbert, what are you bringing to-morrow?'

'Polony sandwiches, Miss, my mum's making 'em, and a bottle of mixed pickles, Miss, home-made!'

Miss Taylor said that would be lovely, and carried on asking right round the class. Tony said

45

that he was bringing a Christmas cake. I was bringing the jelly that my mum was going to make, and Colin Wilkinson was bringing some currant buns. Valerie Burns said that she was bringing some lemon curd tarts, and Freda Holds-worth called her a spiteful cat because *she* was bringing the lemon curd tarts, and Valerie Burns *knew* she was bringing lemon curd tarts because she'd told her and she was a blooming copycat. Anyway Miss Taylor calmed her down by saying that it was a good job they were both bringing lemon curd tarts, because then there would be enough for everybody, and everybody would want one, wouldn't they? And she asked everybody who would want a lemon curd tart to put their hands up, and everybody put their hands up. Even I put my hand up and I hate lemon curd. Well, it *was* Christmas.

After everybody had told Miss Taylor what they were bringing, she said that there'd be enough for the whole school, never mind just our class, but we should remember that Christmas isn't just for eating and parties, and she asked Tony what the most important thing about Christmas is.

'Presents, Miss!'

'No, Tony, not presents. Christmas is when the baby Jesus was born, and that is the most important thing, and when you're all enjoying your presents and parties this year, you must all remember that. Will you all promise me?'

Everybody promised that they'd remember Jesus and then Miss Taylor started asking us all how we were going to spend Christmas. Freda Holdsworth said she was going to Bridlington on Christmas Eve to stay with her cousin, and on Christmas Eve they'd both put their stockings up for Father Christmas, but before they'd go to bed, they'd leave a glass of milk and some biscuits for him in case he was hungry. Norbert Lightowler said that that's daft because there's no such thing as Father Christmas. Some of the others agreed, but most of them said course there is. I just wasn't sure. What I can't understand is, that if there *is* a Father Christmas, how does he get round everybody in one night? I mean the presents must come from somewhere, but how can he do it all by himself? And Norbert said how can there be only *one* Father Christmas, when he'd seen *two* down in town in Baldwin Street and another outside the fish market, and Neville Bastowe said he'd seen one in Dickenson's. Well, what about the one my mum had taken me to see at the Co-op? He'd promised to bring me a racer.

'Please, Miss, there's one at the Co-op an'

all. He's promised to bring me a racer.'

And then Miss Taylor explained that all these others are Father Christmas's brothers and relations who help out because he's so busy and Freda Holdsworth said Miss Taylor was right, and Norbert said he'd never thought of that, but that Paul Hopwood, he's in 2B, had told him that Father Christmas is just his dad dressed up, and I said that that's daft and it couldn't be because Father Christmas comes to our house every year and I haven't got a dad, and Miss Taylor said that if those who didn't believe in Father Christmas didn't get any presents, they'd only have themselves to blame, and I agreed! Then she asked me what I'd be doing on Christmas Day.

'Well, Miss, when I wake up in the morning, I'll look round and see what presents I've got, and I'll play with them and I'll empty my stocking, and usually there are some sweets so I'll eat them, and when I've played a bit more I'll go and wake my mum up and show her what I've got, and then I'll wake my Auntie Doreen – she always stays with us every Christmas; and then after breakfast I'll play a bit more, and then we'll have Christmas dinner, and then we'll go to my grandad's and I'll play a bit more there, and then I'll go home to bed, and that'll be the end!'

48

Miss Taylor said that all sounded very nice and she hoped everybody would have such a nice Christmas, but she was surprised I wasn't going to church. Well, I told her that there wouldn't really be time because my grandad likes us to be there early to hear Wilfred Pickles on the wireless visiting a hospital, and to listen to the Queen talking, and then the bell went for home-time and Miss Taylor said we could all go quietly and told us not to forget our stuff for the party.

I went with Tony to get our coats from the cloakroom. Everybody was talking about the party and Barry was there shouting out that their class was going to have the best table because their teacher had made them a Christmas pudding with money in it! I told him that was nothing because Miss Taylor had given everybody in our class sixpence, but he didn't believe me.

'Gerraway, you bloomin' fibber.'

'She did, didn't she, Tony?'

Tony shook his head.

'Did she heckers like – she wouldn't give 'owt away.'

Huh! You'd think Tony'd've helped me kid Barry along.

'Well, she bought all our Christmas decorations for the classroom . . .' and I went to get my coat.

I took my gloves out of my pocket and they were still soaking wet from snowballing at playtime, so I thought I'd put them on the pipes to dry.

'Hey, Tony, my gloves are still sodden.'

'Well put 'em on the pipes.'

'Yeh, that's a good idea.'

While they dried I sat on the pipes. Ooh, it was lovely and warm. There's a window above the basins and I could see the snow was still coming down, really thickly now.

'Hey, it isn't half going to be deep tomorrow.'

Everybody had gone now except for Barry, Tony and me. Tony was standing on the basins looking out of the window and Barry was doing up his coat. It has a hood on it. I wish I had one like it. I could see through the door into the main hall where the Christmas tree was. It looked lovely. Ever so big. It was nearly up to the ceiling.

'Hey, isn't it a big Christmas tree?' Tony jumped down from the basin and came over to where I was sitting.

'Yeh. It's smashing. All them coloured balls. Isn't it lovely, eh, Barry?'

Barry came over.

'Not bad. C'mon you two, let's get going, eh?'

'Just a sec, let's see if my gloves are dry.'

They weren't really but I put them on. As I

was fastening my coat, Barry said how about going carol singing to get a bit of money.

Tony was quite keen, but I didn't know. I mean my mum'd be expecting me home round about now.

'I suppose *you* can't come because your mum'll be cross with you, as usual!'

Huh. It's all right for Barry. His mum and dad aren't bothered where he goes.

'Course I'll come. Where do you want to go?'

Barry said down near the woods where the posh live, but Tony said it was useless there because they never gave you nowt. So we decided to go round Belgrave Road way, where it's only *quite* posh. It takes about ten minutes to get to Belgrave Road from our school and on the way we argued about which carols to sing. I wanted *Away in a Manger* but Barry wanted *O Come all Ye Faithful*.'

'*Away in a Manger* isn't half as good as *O Come all Ye Faithful*, is it, Tony?'

Tony shrugged his shoulders.

'I quite like *Once in Royal David's City*.'

In the end we decided to take it in turns to choose. Belgrave Road's ever so long and we started at number three with *O Come all Ye Faithful*.

'O come all ye faithful, joyful and trium . . .'

That was as far as we got. A bloke opened the door, gave us three halfpence and told us to push off.

Tony was disgusted.

'That's a good start, halfpenny each.'

Barry told him to stop grumbling.

'It's better than nothing. C'mon.'

We went on to number five and Tony and Barry started quarrelling again because Tony said it was his turn to choose, but Barry wanted his go again because we'd only sung one line. So we did *O Come all Ye Faithful* again.

'Oh come all ye faithful, joyful and triumphant, Oh . . .'

We didn't get any further this time either. An old lady opened the door and said her mother was poorly so could we sing a bit quieter. We started once more but she stopped us again and said it was still just a little bit too loud and could we sing it quieter.

'O come all ye faithful, joyful and triumphant, O come ye, o come ye to Be-eth-lehem . . .'

And we sang the whole thing like that, in whispers. We could hardly hear each other. I felt daft and started giggling and that set Tony and Barry off, but the old lady didn't seem to notice.

She just stood there while we sang and when we finished she said thank you and gave us twopence each.

At the next house we sang *Once in Royal David's City* right through and then rang the door-bell, but nobody came. We missed number nine out because it was empty and up for sale, and at number eleven we sang *Away in a Manger*.

We went to the end of the road singing every carol we knew. We must've made about a pound between us by the time we got to the other end, and Barry said how about going back and doing the other side of the road. I was all for it, but I just happened to see St Chad's clock. Bloomin' heck! Twenty to nine! I couldn't believe it. I thought it'd be about half-past six, if that. Twenty to nine!

'Hey, I'd better get going. It's twenty to nine. My mum'll kill me!'

The other two said they were going to do a bit more carol singing, so they gave me my share of the money and I ran home as fast as I could. I took a short cut through the snicket behind the fish and chip shop and I got home in about five minutes. I could see my mum standing outside the front door talking to Mrs Theabould, our next door neighbour. She saw me and walked towards me. I tried to act all calm as if it was only about half-past five or six o'clock.

'Hello, Mum, I've been carol singing.'

She gave me a clout. She nearly knocked me over. Right on my freezing cold ear an' all.

'Get inside, you! I've been going mad with worry. Do you know what time it is? Nine o'clock. Get inside!'

She pushed me inside and I heard her thank Mrs Theabould and come in after me. I thought she was going to give me another clout, but she just shouted at me, saying that I was lucky she didn't get the police out, and why didn't I tell her where I was? By this time I was crying my head off.

'But I was only bloomin' carol singing.'

'I'll give you carol singing. Get off to bed,' and she pushed me upstairs into my bedroom.

'But what about my jelly for tomorrow? Have you made it?'

I thought she was going to go mad.

'Jelly! I'll give you jelly. If you think I've nothing better to do than make jellies while you're out roaming the streets! Get to bed!'

'But I've told Miss Taylor I'm bringing a jelly. I've got to have one. Please, Mum.'

54

She just told me to wash my hands and face and get to bed.

'And if I hear another word out of you, you'll get such a good hiding, you'll wish you hadn't come home,' and she went downstairs.

I didn't dare say another word. What was I going to do about my jelly? I had to bring one. I'd promised. There was only one thing for it. I'd have to make one myself. So I decided to wait until my mum went to bed, and then I'd go downstairs and make one. I don't know how I kept awake. I'm sure I nodded off once or twice, but after a while I heard my mum switch her light out, and when I'd given her enough time to get to sleep, I crept downstairs.

I've seen my mum make jellies tons of times and I knew you had to have boiling water, so I put the kettle on. I looked in the cupboard for a jelly and at first I thought I'd had it, but I found one and emptied it into a glass bowl. It was a funny jelly. Not like the ones my mum usually has. It was sort of like a powder. Still, it said jelly on the packet, so it was all right. A new flavour most likely. I poured the hot water into a bowl, closed the cupboard door, switched off the light, and took the jelly upstairs and I put it under my bed. I could hear my mum snoring so I knew I was all right, and I went to sleep.

Next thing I heard was my mum shouting from downstairs.

'C'mon, get up or you'll be late for school.'

I got up and pulled the jelly from under the bed. It had set lovely. All wobbly. But it was a bit of a funny colour, sort of yellowy-white. Still I'd got my jelly and that's what mattered. My mum didn't say much when I got downstairs. She just told me to eat my breakfast and get to school, so I did. When I'd finished I put my coat on and said tarah to my mum in the kitchen and went off. But first I sneaked upstairs and got my jelly and wrapped it in a piece of newspaper.

The first thing we had to do at school was to take what we'd brought for the party into the main hall and stick on a label with our name on it and leave it on our table. Norbert Lightowler was there with his polony sandwiches and mixed pickles. So was Neville Bastowe. Neville Bastowe said that my jelly was a bit funny looking, but Norbert said he loved jelly more than anything else and he could eat all the jellies in the world. Miss Taylor came along then and told us to take our coats off and go to our classroom. The party wasn't starting till twelve o'clock, so in the

56

morning we played games and sang carols and Miss Taylor read us a story.

Then we had a long playtime and we had a snowball fight with 2B, and I went on the slides until old Wilkie, that's the caretaker, came and put ashes on the ice. Then the bell went and we all had to go to our tables in the main hall. At every place was a Christmas cracker, and everybody had a streamer, but Mr Dyson, the Headmaster, said that we couldn't throw any streamers until we'd finished eating. I pulled my cracker with Tony and got a red paper hat and a pencil sharpener. Tony got a blue hat and a small magnifying glass. When everybody had pulled their crackers we said grace and started eating. I started with a sausage roll that Neville Bastowe had brought, and a polony sandwich.

Miss Taylor had shared my jelly out in bowls and Jennifer Greenwood said it looked horrible and she wasn't going to have any. So did Freda Holdsworth. But Norbert was already on his jelly and said it was lovely and he'd eat anybody else's. Tony started his jelly and spat it out.

'Ugh, it's horrible.'

I tasted mine, and it *was* horrible, but I forced it down.

'It's not that bad.'

Just then Tony said he could see my mum.

'Isn't that your mum over there?'

He pointed to the door. She was talking to Miss Taylor and they both came over.

'Your mother says you forgot your jelly this morning, here it is.'

Miss Taylor put a lovely red jelly on the table. It had bananas and cream on it, and bits of orange. My mum asked me where I'd got my jelly from. I told her I'd made it. I thought she'd be cross, but she and Miss Taylor just laughed and told us to enjoy ourselves, and then my mum went off. Everybody put their hands up for a portion of my mum's jelly – except Norbert.

'I don't want any of that. This is lovely. What flavour is it?'

I told him it was a new flavour and I'd never heard of it before.

'Well, what's it called?'

'Aspic.'

'Y'what?'

'Aspic jelly – it's a new flavour!'

59

Norbert ate the whole thing and was sick afterwards, and everybody else had some of my mum's. It was a right good party.

This story is by George Layton.

Loving and Giving

'Christmas is a time for giving as well as getting.'
Every child knows that; even two and three year
olds are initiated into secret buyings and wrapping
ups; all autumn, children spend hours in making
things, those heavy-as-lead carpentry gifts (mother
and father paying for the wood), raffia mats,
cross-stitch kettle-holders, embroidery, home
bound books. 'You must not only give, you must
love to give,' our mother insisted, and in spite of
the work it was easy to love this planning and
spending; but when it came to giving away our
own presents, presents we had been given, it was

quite another idea and in our Indian childhood it seemed exceedingly hard that we, four sisters, were never allowed to keep a single thing from any of the Christmas 'dollies'.

'A 'dolly' – I must explain – was not a doll; it was the name given to the baskets of gifts brought on Christmas morning by Indian merchants, contractors and head members of the office staffs as compliments to their Christian clients and employers.

It had become a custom, and custom had built up a ritual for it. The dollies were not handed over in the offices; they were presents and had to be presented with Indian courtesy which meant that every giver had to call personally at each house and make his salaams.

For the merchants and babus it must have been an arduous and expensive morning – for us it was a training in patience and obedience. My father and mother received on the front verandah; Mahommed Shah, our Big Mahommedhan butler, regulated the queue, announcing each visitor in turn. Perhaps it would be one of my father's own babus resplendent in snow-white muslin shirt and dhoti – the long flowing cloth worn draped as a nether garment – coloured socks and sock suspenders, patent leather pumps; perhaps it was a Marwari, one of the merchants or stockbrokers, usually rich and dressed in a cream silk achkan – a long tunic coat – marigold-coloured turban, a fresh scarlet tika mark on his forehead. A tika mark is the small red spot painted between the eyebrows, put on by the priest after ritual bathing. Sometimes a Marwari would bring his children, they were in European clothes except for round velvet hats like pill-box lids embroidered in gold. They had gold earrings too, and smelled strongly of coconut oil. At once an unspoken bond would spring up between us and them – the dolly things were not for them either.

The ritual was always the same: my father was garlanded, sometimes my mother; in a minute or so the long necklaces of jessamine or marigold flowers would be taken off and coiled on a tray held by Abdul, our officious nursery servant – Abdul had always to be in on everything – and as the morning went on the pyramid of garlands grew into a scented mountain. The caller was seated and five minutes would be spent in polite conversation. We children were not often brought into the foreground or the conversation – my father and mother had no son and the calamity of four daughters, all of whom would presumably have to be dowried, was better ignored – but there was plenty to interest us; during the talk, the baskets were carried in by the caller's servants and put down at my father's feet.

Dollies were always in light round baskets, of

the sort coolies use, but now decorated with flowers and sheets of coloured paper. Sometimes there was only one, sometimes two or three, their number and cost depending on the richness of the giver, and the importance of my father's patronage to him; sometimes it was in genuine gratitude for help in the past year, but the giver knew, as my father knew – as everyone in India knew – that there was a code of strict limitation on the cost.

In the old East India Company days dollies were often bribes – and fabulous bribes. This suspicion of bribery still hung over them and anything gold or silver, even children's bangles, was immediately handed back; there could be none of the exquisite gauze and gold thread saris or scarves that came from Benares; a bottle of whisky or a length of plain silk was the utmost limit. Usually there were only flowers, fruit, cakes, sweets and, for us children, crackers and toys.

In spite of the semi-royal state in which the English in India lived, we were brought up quite frugally, not too much of anything, certainly not many toys and we yearned after those dollies. Certainly, I have never seen anything more attractive: the foundation was always fruit; red apples from Kulu, bananas – sometimes a whole stem of them was carried in and set beside the basket as an extra – papayas, pommelloes like big pink fleshed grapefruit, tangerines in silver paper, nuts. To one side would be a Christmas cake, florid with shop icing, which we thought wonderful – our cake was home-made. There would be a box of chocolates tied with ribbon – sometimes four boxes of chocolates for four sisters, never to be allowed to keep them. There were Indian sweets, jillipis, clear spiral rings of toffee sugar – or sandesh, which was a sort of fudge stuck with silver paper. Crackers and toys were poised on top. We duly had to thank for them; the caller airily waved his hand and said 'They are nothing, nothing,' though they must have cost him many rupees. He then made way for the next visitor and the baskets were spirited away.

Not entirely spirited. They were taken to the dining-room, which in our Indian-built home was as large as a ballroom; there Nan, our Eurasian nurse, and our Ayah, unpacked them and arranged them on the dining-room table in pyramids of fruit, platters of sweets, rows of cakes, piles of crackers; the toys were heaped on the floor. As soon as the last caller had gone from the front verandah, the last car or tikka gharri – little box-like carriages drawn by two ponies – driven away, a familiar, shuffling, rustling, whispering, giggling and sniffling began on the back verandah. The noise grew louder until Mahommed Shah threw open the door and in came the droves of the servants' children.

We were not rich people but we must have had something like eighteen servants then, Christian, Mahommedhan, Hindus of all castes and there were between sixty and eighty children including the dhobi's (washerman's) clan, now mysteriously swelled to double size – but my mother never sent any of the little gate-crashers away. Some we knew well as they lived in the compound; some, like Mahommed Shah's, who had a house nearly as large as ours, came only at Christmas. Some were our enemies – there had been scuffles and ambushes – some our dear friends, but now one would have thought we had never met before; we of the back verandah were quite as ceremonious as our elders of the front. There were, of course, no garlands but the children gave us salaams which we gravely returned.

The protocol was strict: Mahommed Shah's big girl and small boys stood near the table – they in clean shirts and dhotis, she in a Punjabi, the loose tunic and trousers, with a little gauze head or breast scarf worn by Mahommedhan girls. All the gardeners' children stood apart; they were Bhramins, the priestly caste, the small girls were exquisite in saris, jessamine flowers in their hair. The dhobi's children were everywhere, some of them dressed only in a charm string and short cotton jacket that left their rice swollen stomachs and private parts bare; the babies wore nothing at all except charm strings, but they were oiled all over. Far over by the door stood the sweeper's son and behind him a smaller boy who, unlike other children, was employed. He had the curious task – for which, touchingly, he would put on his only shirt – of being fetched in to pick up and carry away the bodies of any dead crows that fell into the garden or any casualties among our guinea pigs. No other servant would or could touch a corpse, not even of a pet.

This protocol was not of our seeking; we were often companions of the sweeper's boy – he could fly our kites from the roof better than any of us – but we knew that now, as an untouchable, he must keep apart, just as we knew that the gardeners' children must not be given fruit or cakes or sweets; they would not be allowed to eat them because non-Bhramini hands had touched them, non-Bhramini shadows fallen on them, not only non-Bhramini; by Hindu ruling we, as western children, were untouchables as well. It was all part of the intricate web of rules and taboos that govern the whole of Indian social life: children could usually break through it, but not today. This was a public occasion.

'Can't we keep that *darling* little doll? One little basket of cooking pots? One box of chocolates?' But we never could. The answer was always the same and it was the four of us who were required to do the actual giving, acting as reluctant little Lady Bountifuls. My youngest sister Rose was a greedy child and Nan sometimes had literally to prise a drum of Turkish delight or a box of chocolates out of her hand.

We parted first with the fruit and nuts; these were tied swiftly into the corners of saris or dhotis or collected by the dhobi's wife into an old pillow case. (The dhobi's wife always fascinated us because she had elephantiasis. We stared at her gargantuan feet and ankles.) Then each of the children was given an empty cracker box or its lid to hold. These were filled with sweets; the boxes of chocolates were ripped open or given whole to a family. Then the Christmas cakes were allotted and this was done in the unfair way of the world – the largest and best cakes to the richest children, the worst to the neediest, but my mother always kept a collection of inconspicuous pink iced cakes to help fill the maws of the small dhobis. At last came the moment for which everyone was really waiting – the distribution of the toys.

Why was it such a pang to part with these? Why did we like them so much? I suppose because no-one else ever gave such things to us. We each had a sensible gift from our father and mother, probably something we had wanted all the year; in the evening we should each get something from the Club Christmas tree, but in this isolated place the dollies brought the only toys we saw from outside the great world, as it were. Some were Indian; miniature brass cooking pots, platters and ladles, or wooden animals, miniature too and painted with spots and red daisies which made them look seductive and all packed in small chip baskets; there were glass bangles in jewel colours which we were not allowed to wear; wonderfully cut paper balls; clay gods and goddesses; and with these were western toys, one for each of us: cheap clockwork cars and trains, wooden animals that clacked and bounced, celluloid toys, dolls with fixed eyes, gummed on clothes, chip straw hats. Here again, the rich had the best: Mahommed Shah's daughter the most splendiferous doll – the dhobi's the collection of celluloids, but immediately after came the crackers as consolation. Crackers were always divided equally.

People say crackers are expensive nonsense. I wish they could have seen those children with them. 'A-aah! A-aah! Aie! Aie!' Murmurs broke out all over the room. The big kohl-darkened eyes grew bigger, brown faces broke into smiles; the small brown hands holding the cardboard box trays trembled. Those crackers would be kept long after the things inside had been taken out; the gaudy fringed papers, the least tinselled star be made a treasure. We liked giving the crackers – by then we had been won over and nothing mattered except that the children should be made as contented as possible; but then the ritual was finished. In a few minutes the last child had salaamed and scurried away; the baskets were picked up empty. Once again everything was gone.

'Look where those children live, and look where you . . .' Nan would scold. We knew quite well where they lived, mostly in a line of brick-built rooms behind the cookhouse, one room to a family, one tap to a whole row. The dhobi children lived in the wash court, the grooms in a wicker hut beside the stable, but we did not see anything wrong with this. Indeed, it seemed gloriously simple; no nursery or schoolroom, no coming down to the dining-room for meals, no changing to go into the drawing-room, so few clothes; and to us those little rooms were home-like, with their swept earth floors, clay oven, shelf of brass cooking pots, perhaps a day bed, the straw sleeping mats rolled up, the family posses-sions in a tin trunk painted with roses, the family umbrella hanging from the rafters. The poorer the house, the prettier, because it did not have such uglinesses as aluminium saucepans, army blankets, china plates, petrol lamps. The children ate off banana leaves with their fingers. At night the soft flicker of a wick floating in an earthenware lamp turned all the walls to gold. 'You are so lucky,' Nan always said. They were lucky too. 'And I don't see,' Rose said obstinately, 'why they should have our toys.'

'You wouldn't want to keep all those?'

'I would.' Rose was firm. She was young enough to say what she thought unabashed, but we could only feel; the fact that we knew we were selfish only made it worse.

'You must not only give, you must love

giving.' Perhaps that early training grew into our bones. I do love to give, yet still, somewhere, at the back of my mind is an unsatisfied yearning and I wish that somehow, something that can never happen in far off England would happen, and I could have one dolly entirely to myself.

This story is by Rumer Godden.

A Lot of Mince-pies

I wish to God I'd never heard of the school choir, and I'm not the only one. In three days' time we'll go carolling round the village, same as every year. We'll work our melodious way along the High Street, trekking up gravel driveways to do our stuff and knock for donations. All proceeds to local charities. We'll do all the posh houses on Micklebarrow Close, then the Red Lion and the supermarket car-park. The supermarket'll be open late and seething with last-minute shoppers as it always is on Christmas Eve. We never fail to make a killing there. And after that we'll move out to where the street-lamps end and do some of the cottages and a farm or two. The cottages are a dead loss as far as money's concerned, but school choirs have sung outside them since just after the dinosaurs and we carry on the tradition. The farms are better. They know we're coming so they keep the dogs in and do hot mince-pies and ginger wine for us. I can't stand mince-pies.

Anyway, from the minute we troop out of the schoolyard behind old Exley at seven o'clock, the kids'll be waiting for one thing. They'll be waiting for the last house – the Meltons' place, with its tangled garden, crumbling brick, and funny little windows. It's three-quarters of a mile from the village, and the choir usually gets there about nine o'clock. The Meltons'll be waiting, and as soon as we strike up the first number they'll open the door and stand there in carpet-slippers, smiling and swaying a little to the music. They're the most ancient couple you're ever likely to see – my mum says they were old when she was in the choir – but the thing about them is, you can actually see that they're enjoying the carols, and afterwards they make a generous donation and give presents to all the kids. There's always eighteen in the choir and I suppose the Meltons buy the stuff on their Christmas shopping expedition, but I don't know where they go – nobody ever sees them in the village. The presents aren't tatty either – none of your quid-a-dozen made in Taiwan plastic rubbish. They tend to be things like cartridge pens, penknives and wallets and purses made of real leather. Last year I got a calculator. As soon as the singing's over they beckon some kid inside – someone whose face they've taken a fancy to I suppose – and the chosen one reappears a few minutes later with a double armful of little packets.

By now you'll be thinking this sounds like the perfect end to Christmas Eve and wondering why I'm moaning. Hang about, and I'll tell you what happened last year.

It was a clear, starry night, and the hoar-frost was already forming on the grass as we left the last of the farms behind and set off to sing for the Meltons. The fields were sheets of silver and the hedges were black and I slackened my pace till a gap opened between me and the others. It was very still and quiet, and suddenly I got this feeling that once, on a frosty night long ago, somebody like me had passed this way alone. I don't know what brought it on but it was a heck of a strong feeling – like being haunted without actually seeing anything. I shivered, and then a wave of sadness hit me for that unknown walker, long since dead. It must have been the quiet that did it – that or the moonlight. Anyway it rattled me, and I was glad when Shaun Wrigley noticed I wasn't with the party and turned, shouting to me to get a move on.

We got to the Meltons' place at ten past nine. One downstairs window strained pale light through its curtain but the garden was black. The gate had no top hinge and old Exley had to lift it before he could open it. It squealed, and when he dropped it there were glove-prints in its coating of frost.

Beyond the gate, some sunflowers had blown over. Their dried-out heads hung low across the path. They nodded and crackled as we waded through them. One snapped off and Shaun Wrigley booted it. It cartwheeled up the path shedding seeds, then veered off into long grass. We formed an arc around the door, shuffling and clearing our throats. Our breath hung in clouds round our heads.

'Right, folks?' old Exley whispered. He only called us folks on Christmas Eve. '*Hark the Herald*, after two.' He counted us in and we were away.

They must have been waiting behind the door, because halfway through line three the latch clicked and it swung inwards and there they were, him with his arm round her shoulder, nodding in time with the music. You couldn't tell if they were smiling because what light there was was behind them, but you got the impression that they were.

We went through our repertoire, making a pretty good job of it. My feet got so cold standing still I couldn't feel them, but I didn't mind. It was our last stint, and in ten minutes or so I'd be on my way home with the job behind me for another year and a nice little gift in my pocket.

Our last number was *We Wish You a Merry Christmas*. Nobody could accuse us of originality. As the final note died away, the Meltons clapped. They always did that. Then the old guy flapped a hand and said, 'Let that one come in – the one with the bobble-cap.' We were all bunched together so you couldn't tell who he meant, and I'd forgotten I had my pom-pom hat on so I didn't move. Old Exley craned over the kids' heads, trying to see where old Melton was pointing. He spotted my pom-pom and said, 'Wake up, lad – the gentleman's waiting.'

I hurried forward, feeling myself go red. As I did so this third-year girl, Stephanie Williams, said something I didn't catch and made a half-hearted grab for my sleeve. She had a funny look on her face but she's a peculiar girl at the best of times and I just sort of jerked my arm out of her reach and brushed past. It wasn't till I was inside with my hat in my hand that I remembered Stephanie'd been the chosen one last year.

I was standing in a stone-flagged passageway. To my left a door stood ajar. Light trickled feebly from beyond it, falling in a wedge across the flags. I saw slug-trails and there was a flat, fungoid smell.

The old woman slipped a hand under my elbow and began steering me along the passageway. Beyond the puddle of light I was virtually blind. Behind me, the old man closed the door.

'This way, my dear.' The woman guided me to the foot of some wooden stairs that went up into blackness. I didn't want to insult them or hurt their feelings or anything, but the creepiness of the place was getting to me and I hung back a bit. 'Is there a light?' I ventured.

'Oh, no, dear.' She sounded surprised – shocked, almost. The old man, shuffling after us said, 'He can't do with the light, you see.'

'Who?' My scalp prickled. We began climbing the uncarpeted stairs.

'Why Gilbert of course,' said the woman. 'Our little son. He can't do with it, can he, Daddy?'

'No, Mummy,' her husband replied. 'He's a good boy, but he can't do with the light at all.'

As we ascended the air grew colder and the rank smell more intrusive. The woman's fingers felt like claws in the crook of my elbow, and suddenly I wanted to break free and run for it. I didn't, because the man was right behind us and because I didn't fancy looking like a wally in front of the choir. Instead I said, 'I didn't know you had a boy.' My voice sounded shaky, even to me.

'Oh, yes,' crooned the woman. 'We've had him ever such a long time haven't we, Daddy?'

'A long, long time, Mummy,' old Melton confirmed, and it occurred to me that they were probably mad. It was Christmas Eve and here I was in the dark with a pair of decrepit lunatics who thought they had a kid called Gilbert.

At the top of the stairs was a creaky landing. It was not completely dark, because there was a door with about an inch of bluish light showing under it. Mrs Melton let go my arm and whispered, 'Gilbert's room. I'll open the door, and you can pop in and give him his present.'

'Present?' A mixture of dread and embarrassment scrambled my brain. I had no present. Was

I supposed to have? Perhaps a gift for Gilbert was part of the yearly ritual. If so, nobody'd told me. I flushed in the chill gloom, stammering, 'I – I'm sorry, Mrs Melton. I didn't know. I haven't—'

'Yes, you have.' I started as the old man, who must have crept up behind me, hissed in my ear. His breath smelled vile.

The only thing I had was my hat, now a damp, screwed-up lump in my hands. I remembered he'd mentioned it outside. The one with the bobble cap. Stupidly, I held it out. 'This – you mean this?' He chuckled.

'A kiss,' he whispered. 'Only a kiss, under the mistletoe.'

'I'm a boy,' I croaked, appalled. 'I don't kiss other boys.'

He didn't reply.

The woman stretched up and drew a bolt near the top of the door. It grated and slammed. As the echo died I heard something else – an uncouth, wordless cry from the room beyond, and I knew then that Gilbert was real and that there must be something horribly wrong with him. She bent and drew a second bolt.

I don't know why I didn't turn then and run. I'll never know. I only know I've spent every day since wishing I had.

The door swung inward. 'Gilbert,' the woman crooned. 'Here's somebody with a present for you, darling.' I couldn't see past her. The old man laid an arm across my shoulders and pushed me forward. I was half resisting and he really had to exert pressure. He kept murmuring, 'Come along – come along,' as though he was talking to a stubborn infant. If I'd dug my heels in he wouldn't have stood a chance, but even now a part of me was scared of hurting their feelings. A mistletoe kiss seems such a small thing, and how do you tell parents nicely that the thought of being in the same room with their kid makes you want to throw up, let alone kissing him?

The woman moved aside. There was a bed. Above the bed a dim blue lightbulb burned. Somebody had fastened a sprig of mistletoe to its dusty, fraying flex. The light fell on rumpled sheets, and on the boy they called Gilbert.

I gaped. God knows what I'd been expecting – some slavering, semi-human monster I suppose, but Gilbert was beautiful. I know it's a funny word to use about a boy but he was. He lay, propped on one elbow, looking at me through dark, liquid, lemur's eyes. His tip-tilted nose cast a smudge of shadow across a mobile mouth. His hair fell in a dark cascade to his shoulders, concealing the hand that supported his head. His frame was lean, his pale skin smooth as cream.

Old Melton dropped his hand to the small of my back and pushed gently. 'Go on now, boy – one little kiss, that's all.'

I moved towards the bed, but it wasn't the old man's hand that made me. It was partly relief of course – relief that I wasn't about to touch some unspeakable horror with my lips, but mostly it was Gilbert's eyes. I read a bit once out of a book my mum was reading. It was a romance, and somebody was going on about drowning in someone's eyes. It struck me as daft at the time but now, when I try to figure out why I permitted what happened that night to happen, I remember Gilbert's eyes and I think I know what that writer meant.

Anyway, I found myself standing by the bed and I couldn't tear my eyes away from his. He didn't say anything but he made a motion with his head and I knew he wanted me to kneel down. I felt sick and weak and unreal. As I went down on one knee I was back in infant school, doing the crib scene in the Nativity Play. I was the first shepherd, kneeling at the manger with the star above and Mary and Joseph behind, watching. It only lasted a second, and then Gilbert leant forward and his lips parted and I saw why he couldn't talk. His mouth was crammed with spikes.

I won't go on about it. As soon as I saw that mouth I knew what he was, but by then it was too late. He took what he wanted from me and now I'm one of them, like Stephanie Williams and the other chosen. We all make the trip out to the Melton place once a month – each on a separate night of course. We have to go, or we'd die like everybody else.

I expect you're wondering what it's like. Well, you don't feel that much different really, except you've no energy and the light hurts and you see colours as sort of faded. There're a lot more of us about than you think, by the way – so many that you're bound to know at least one. He'll be pasty-faced and a bit flabby, and not too particular about his clothes. He'll be irritable a lot of the time and he won't smile much. You'll probably wonder what he does for fun, or if he even knows what fun is. You might wonder why he bothers to go on living at all, and he'll certainly wonder himself sometimes. I do.

And I suppose the answer is that life's precious,

and we tend to cling on to it even if we're not enjoying it. Whether I'll feel that way a thousand years from now remains to be seen. A thousand years is a lot of mince-pies.

This story is by Robert Swindells.

The Small Brown Mouse

You might not think that smells would travel round the corners in a mousehole, but you would be wrong. The small brown mouse knows at exactly what angle in the hole to sit so that all the smells from the room beyond are reflected to him, accurately and deliciously. He is safe there, with the roof of the mousehole just above his head, and the sides of it sitting snugly to his shoulders, so that nothing can jump at him suddenly from any direction, and he can see the light from the room shining up the tunnel which generations of his family have polished with their furry flanks. Whichever of his ancestors it was who had been the architect for that mousehole, he had known his business well, and each evening the small brown mouse takes up his position, and his quivering nose-tip explores all the smells that reach him.

In the winter evenings the most exciting of the smells are of cocoa and digestive biscuits. And when he smells those the small brown mouse knows that soon there will be a stir in the room, chairs will be pushed back, someone will say, 'Come on, puss – time you were out', doors will open and shut again, feet will sound on the stairs, light feet first, then heavier feet, and at last the room will be left in the quiet dark, but for the glimmer from what is left of the fire.

This is the moment that the mouse has been waiting for. He comes out of the mousehole and across the floor like the flicker of a shadow, and he has his supper from the crumbs on the carpet, and he is thankful that digestive biscuits are so very brittle, and that the family make so many crumbs.

One evening in the middle of winter, the small brown mouse was sitting just round his particular angle in the mousehole, waiting for his supper. It was cold and frosty outside, and he was hungry, and he hoped the biscuits had been rather more brittle than usual, and the family more careless. He waited and he waited, growing hungrier and hungrier, but also more and more puzzled. For mixed up with the smell of cocoa and digestive biscuits he smelt other, unfamiliar smells, which greatly puzzled even so wise a mouse as he. There was cigarette smoke, of course, and the smell of the fire, and he rather thought someone had been sucking peppermints. But there was a very unusual smell – unusual, that is, for a drawing-room – a fresh keen outdoor smell, a smell that didn't belong to a house at all, and there were other sweeter smells that were foreign to him, and most exciting.

The small feet had gone up to bed a long time ago. The other, heavier feet should have been on their way, but still the light burned and there came the continued sound of voices. What with hunger and curiosity the small brown mouse crept another inch towards the room – and then crept an inch back again, for the cat was still there, the silent presence that turned your legs to water and made your heart sick, the dreadful and inescapable cat.

The mouse was beginning to think he should go back up the mousehole and take his supper off the piece of cheeserind he had stored there, in

case of emergencies, when at last he heard the familiar sounds that he had been waiting for. Chairs scraped across the floor, the cat was called, the front door opened and closed again, the light was extinguished and feet – slow, tired feet – went up the stairs.

The small brown mouse came out of the

mousehole and looked around him. And he forgot all about the digestive biscuits, but sat back on his little haunches, and with bright unwinking eyes he stared his fill.

It was a tree, a tall strong tree, set in a tub at the further end of the room. That was the outdoor smell, though what a tree was doing inside a house the mouse did not know. But he breathed in the sharp sweet smell of its branches, and it reminded him of the wood where, in the sunny summertime, he had sometimes wandered. But this tree was different from all other trees. Its dark green branches were hung and spattered from tip to toe. It burned and glittered and sparkled. It was alive with bright colours that were not fruit nor blossom. And at the top was a figure, half child, half bird, and he knew that it was an angel.

Forgetting how hungry he was the mouse crept forward to investigate this unexpected tree. He climbed carefully over the tub and up among the branches, nosing around backward and forward, smelling and feeling and looking at all the things that he found there. There was a bottle of French perfume, and though it was tightly wrapped and stoppered, his nose discovered it, and it made him feel very romantic and sentimental so that he nearly ran away home up the mousehole, to tell his wife about it right away. But a little higher up there was a cigar, and although there was only a breath of it coming through its silvery case, it was enough to make our mouse feel bold and manly, so that he went higher up still, examining everything as he went.

There were boxes of chocolates and trumpets, balls and oranges, candles, wisps of tinsel, cotton wool snow, tiny shining birds that dipped on the branches as his small weight came on to them, and flaunted bright glittering tails. There were books and boxes of handkerchiefs, and many other things which baffled the mouse completely, so strange and unusual they were. But what he most admired were the large bright balls, red and blue, green and gold, in which, by the light of the fire, he could see his own reflection looking out at him – a warlike red mouse in the red ball, a romantic blue mouse, a mermaid mouse of cool translucent green. Best of all was an amber ball which reflected a tawny benevolent lion of a mouse, a mouse as truly golden as the cheese that mice dream about when they are happiest.

Soon he had been all over the tree, except for the highest branches, where there was little foothold, and where even his feather weight might find little enough support. It was only then that he remembered how hungry he was, and he went down to the carpet again, and ate up the crumbs of the digestive biscuits, and as he chewed he never took his eyes off the splendid tree.

His supper gave him courage, and he decided that after all he would attempt the last perilous inches to the top, where on the slender stem the angel was poised.

So up he went again, scrambling and sliding, and he paused only to look just once more at his golden self, reflected in the amber glass ball. And at last there was only a slim six inches between him and the small white feet of the angel.

But just at the base of the final pinnacle was something that the mouse had not seen in his first excursion, something as small as himself, something in fact very like himself – three chocolate mice. They lay side by side on the very last branch, just beneath the angel, and our mouse looked at them, first with curiosity and then with pity, for they were clumsy things compared with his own exquisite shape. Their ears were no more than humps on either side of their thick heads; their eyes were just spots of white sugar on the chocolate – set on unevenly at that; there wasn't a whisker between them, and their tails were poor things of limp string that hung down behind them. Our mouse looked back at his own elegant tapered tail that kept the balance of his body, and he looked again at the dangling bits of string, and he felt rather ashamed. But he also felt extremely interested, for the smell of the chocolate had reached him so suddenly and so magnificently that he almost lost his balance and fell from his precarious perch.

It was like the smell of cocoa, of course, but so much better, so much richer, that there was really little comparison. The shock of its sweetness paralysed him for a moment, and then he came a little closer, delaying – just for the pure pleasure of delaying – the lovely moment when his tongue should slide up the shining sides of the first mouse.

'No,' said the angel suddenly – so suddenly that the small brown mouse once more had difficulty in keeping his footing – 'No. Not now – not yet – not for you.'

She wasn't scolding, she was just telling him, and she smiled at him as she spoke so that the mouse was at once ashamed of himself. 'Yes ma'am,' he said, and because the chocolate mice still smelt so overpoweringly beautiful – so much so that he could not keep his whiskers from vibrating – he came down off the tree, where the smell of them was mixed up with a lot of other smells, and he finished up a few crumbs of biscuit that he had previously overlooked.

He should then have gone back into the safety of his mousehole, but he could not bring himself to leave the enchanted tree, and all night he sat in front of the fire, watching it.

Even when the last flicker of the fire had burned itself out, and the coals sighed and fell together in white ash on the hearth, the mouse still sat on, for of course a mouse can see in the dark, and this mouse had never seen anything like this before. He forgot his wife who was waiting for him, he forgot to count the hours striking on the big clock in the hall, he forgot everything except the tree. That was why, when morning had come he was still sitting there when the mistress of the house opened the door – and the cat walked in! Before he knew it the great cat was coming softly and steadily across the hearth towards him, and the mouse knew that he was lost indeed.

The cat sat down placidly, a few feet away, and made no spring. The mouse watched him, sick with fear, unable to move. He wished the cat would be quick and spring, and make a finish to it.

'Hallo, nipper,' said the great animal, and the mouse saw his strong white pointed teeth as he spoke, 'don't be in a hurry to move. You needn't mind me.'

And still he didn't spring.

'I'm not going to chase you,' the cat said. And for some reason that he could not explain the mouse believed the cat, just as he had believed the angel.

'Why not?' he asked, trying to keep the wobble out of his voice.

'I don't know exactly,' the cat replied, blinking a mild yellow eye, 'but it's a thing we always do at this time of year. Traditional, you know.'

The mouse didn't know, but a warm gratitude made it impossible for him to speak.

'Mind you,' the cat went on, 'I shall chase you tomorrow, and every other day that I get the chance. Like as not I shall catch you too. But not today.' And he busied himself licking the pads of his great paws, keeping the claws politely hooded.

The mouse believed this too. He knew that the cat would indeed chase him tomorrow and every other day, but he also knew that after this it would always be different. He would be able to run away from the cat now, because he knew that the cat was just another animal, as he himself was an animal – a much stronger animal of course, but just an animal: not a horror that turned your legs

to water and made your heart sick. Oh yes, he
could run away from the cat now. Out of sheer
bravado he crept across the few feet that lay
between the cat and himself, and he leaned for a
small daring moment against the cat's side, and
felt the warmth and power of his great body. That
would be something to tell his wife about when
he got home.

Then the house began to stir, there were
laughter and voices, people came and went, the

cat was called for his breakfast – and the small brown mouse, who was by this time so excited that he hardly knew what he was doing, instead of running to his mousehole and safety, streaked for the tree, and lay hidden among its branches and saw all that was going on.

There was plenty to see. Visitors arrived all day long. They greeted each other, and laughed, and opened parcels, and kissed, and sang. And in the evening they drew the curtains across the windows, and they lighted the candles on the tree.

This was something so alarming that the mouse, between the striking of one match and the next, fled up the tree where there were no candles, and found himself lying once again beside his chocolate cousins.

When all the candles were lit, the parcels were untied from the tree, and handed down into small excited hands, and the mouse, from his point of vantage, looked down on the children's upturned faces. Then it was the turn for the grown-up people to receive their parcels, and at last each pair of hands was filled.

There was nothing left on the tree now, except the angel and the candles and the bright balls – oh, and the chocolate mice. 'I'd forgotten about these,' someone said, and a hand reached up and up, among the branches.

There was no hope for it – he would be discovered. But just as the fingers fumbled for the chocolate mice, the angel's golden wing tilted ever so slightly, and the small brown mouse was safely sheltered behind it. There he lay, hidden and safe, until the party was over, until people had said goodbye, until the door had opened many times and shut again, until the candles were blown out and the light extinguished, and until the last of the feet had once more gone up the stairs and the house was quiet.

Suddenly it all seemed rather sad. Even the tree looked a little sad. The mouse thought of all the hands that had gone home full of treasures, and he felt sad, too – sad, and also tremendously tired.

'I'll go now,' he said to the angel, 'and thank you, ma'am, for helping me.'

And he got slowly down off the tree – he was stiff with lying so long in one position – and he crossed the room to the mousehole. Just before he went home he turned to the tree, for one last look.

'You are sad,' the angel said. 'What is the matter?'

He found it difficult to explain. 'You said.

"Not yet – not now",' he faltered, 'but the party is over.'

Just then the amber ball slid off the twig that held it, softly down from one branch to another, gently to the ground, and it rolled to his feet and stopped there.

The mouse looked up at the angel questioningly. 'For me?' And the angel smiled and nodded.

You might not think that a bright ball from a Christmas tree would travel round the corners in a mousehole. But you would be wrong.

This story is by Janet McNeill.

The Twelfth-Night King

'Twelfth Night' (or the Feast of the Epiphany) is on January 6th and commemorates the visit of the Wise Men from the East to the infant Saviour. One of the chief things in a Twelfth Night festival was a cake with a bean buried in it. Whoever was lucky enough to get the slice of cake which had the bean in it was made bean-king and was master of the revels.

The custom of choosing a 'one day King' was a very old one though usually the choice made was not so happy as that told of in the story which follows.

As far as little Pierre Porcher was concerned, it had been a very lean Christmas, that Christmas of

1364, in fact no Christmas at all. He had gone to the midnight mass with his mother, and seen the crèche in the great church, but as for having presents, or good things to eat, he had never heard of such things in all the eight years of his life.

Pierre was always cold and hungry in the winter, for he was very poor. He and his mother lived in a wretched little hut just outside the ancient city of Moulins, in central France.

All day long Pierre tended pigs in the fields, and never dreamt of going to school, for his peasant father had been killed in the wars, and, since that time, his poor mother had worked so hard that she had often been ill. Between them, they had been barely able to eke out an existence.

One cold and snowy morning, the day before Twelfth Day, or the Festival of the Epiphany, several squires of the Duke of Bourbon, who lived in the great château above Moulins, were seen busily riding about the city and its neighbourhood. In answer to the call of one of these horsemen, the door of a hovel beside the road opened, and a peasant woman, poorly dressed, and shod with wooden shoes, appeared.

'Is this the residence of the widow Porcher?' said the squire, with mock politeness, and the woman nodded in open-mouthed astonishment.

'I have news for thee, my good dame,' continued the man. 'Listen to the order of good Duke Louis. He has commanded us to make a search among the poorest houses of the city for a boy of eight years. Him the Duke wishes to borrow for one day, that he may entertain him at the château. Know, then, that we have done you the honour of selecting your little son. He will be returned to you unharmed.'

The widow Porcher's surprise was profound. At first she thought it was all a heartless joke, but the squire showed her the order written upon parchment, and, although the poor woman could not read it, the ducal seal which hung from it could not be mistaken.

Little Pierre, whose curiosity had drawn him to his mother's side, heard the strange order. At the thought of his mother giving him up to the terrible lord who lived in the château, he was so frightened that he could not even cry. He saw the sharp towers of the castle rising against the sky, and would have run away, but his mother held him back, and when she was assured that no harm would come to him, consented to his going.

So Pierre, terrified and struggling, was led away by the horseman, and was soon seated before him on the saddle-bow, riding off to the good Duke Louis.

The next day, in the grand hall of the château, a table of honour was set for the feast of the Twelfth-Night King. Amid a flourish of trumpets, and cheers from the assembled company of nobles, ladies and squires, a child entered, arrayed in a gorgeous mantle embroidered with jewels. Officers and servants surrounded him on every hand. On his right, a page bore the crown, upon

a cushion covered with cloth of gold; a sergeant-at-arms held the mace; the royal falconer had a hooded bird upon his wrist; while the captain of the men-at-arms and the chamberlain assisted the child to his place in the great armchair at the head of the table.

Would you believe it? This child was none other than little Pierre, the swineherd, whom Duke Louis had made King of the Feast. How his eyes grew big before the decorations of that wonderful table, the brilliancy of the silver centre-piece, the heaped dishes of sweetmeats, the gold and silver drinking cups!

The savoury odours of cooked meats, of the great cake kept warm upon a brazier, of the gorgeous peacock, served upon a pasty, in all the glory of his feathers, went to his head, and before these riches the poor little fellow who had never tasted any food except black bread, sat as though entranced.

At one end of the hall was the great fireplace, where roared a blazing fire that threw out warmth and cheer. At the other end, upon a raised platform, before an arched, stained-glass window, the nobles of the surrounding country and their ladies were gathered. In the centre, covered with a canopy, was a dais, on which sat the good Duke

Louis. While all were making merry, his steward approached and presented a silver plate, upon which the Duke put a purse of gold coins for the 'poor king', and to this principal gift all the barons added theirs, until there was a substantial sum. In a corner of the great hall, upon a stone balcony, a band of musicians were waiting for the signal, and during the feast they played sweet music.

Little Pierre was at first so frightened and astonished that he could scarcely eat, but hunger soon brought him to his senses, and he did as every healthy boy does at Christmas time – stuffed himself with good things. You may be sure that his table manners were awkward and uncouth, but there were many to help him and tell him what to do.

When his appetite was fully satisfied, he was led to the grand dais and seated on his throne beside the Duke. Then the tables were cleared away, and there followed dancing and games, songs by troubadours, and tricks and acrobatic feats by the jongleurs and players, while all the time the jester in cap and bells made the hall ring with laughter at his quips and antics.

All this the dazed little king watched from his throne, as in a golden dream.

But, like all dreams, there came the awakening,

and the next morning Pierre found himself in the old hut by the roadside, but no longer cold and cheerless, for the kind squires who brought him back had brought his mother the coins given by the Duke and his court. It was a little fortune to the happy woman, enough to keep her in comfort and to send Pierre to school. How she wept and laughed over him, and called down blessings upon the good Duke!

Whether Pierre became a prosperous merchant or skilful craftsman, we do not know, but whatever his fortune, it is not likely that he ever forgot his one day's reign as the 'Twelfth-Night King'.

This is a true story. For in a very old book called *The Chronicle of the Good Duke of Bourbon*, written by Jehan Cabaret in the fourteenth century, you will find the following statement:

'*In this month of January, 1365, came the Day of the Kings, on which the Duke of Bourbon, dwelling then in his good city of Moulins, held a great fête, and made king of it a child of eight years, the poorest that could be found in all the city. He clothed him in royal garments, and loaned to him all his officers to wait upon him, and made good cheer for this little king, in reverence to God. And the next day this little king dined at the table of honour, after which there came the steward, who took a collection for him. Duke*

Louis de Bourbon gave forty livres to keep him in school, and all the chevaliers of the court each gave a franc, and the esquires each a half-franc. So the sum amounted to no less than a hundred francs, which they gave to the lad's mother. And this beautiful custom the valiant Duke Louis de Bourbon kept up as long as he lived.'

This story is by C. G. Leland.

The Christmas Apple

Once on a time there lived in Germany a little clock-maker by the name of Hermann Joseph. He lived in one little room with a bench for his work, and a chest for his wood, and his tools, and a cupboard for dishes, and a trundle-bed under the bench. Besides these there was a stool, and that was all – excepting the clocks. There were hundreds of clocks: little and big, carved and plain, some with wooden faces and some with porcelain ones – shelf clocks, cuckoo clocks, clocks with chimes and clocks without: and they all hung on the walls, covering them quite up. In front of his one little window there was a little shelf, and on this Hermann put all his best clocks to show passers-by. Often they would stop and look and someone would cry:

'See, Hermann Joseph has made a new clock. It is finer than any of the rest!'

Then if it happened that anybody was wanting a clock he would come in and buy it.

I said Hermann was a little clock-maker. That was because his back was bent and his legs were crooked, which made him very short and funny to look at. But there was no kinder face than his in all the city, and the children loved him. Whenever a toy was broken or a doll had lost an arm or a leg or an eye, its careless mütterchen would carry it straight to Hermann's little shop.

'The kindlein needs mending,' she would say. 'Canst thou do it now for me?'

And whatever work Hermann was doing he would always put it aside to mend the broken toy or doll, and never a pfennig would he take for the mending.

'Go spend it for sweetmeats, or, better still, put it by till Christmas-time. 'Twill get thee some happiness then, maybe,' he would always say.

Now it was the custom in that long ago for those who lived in the city to bring gifts to the great cathedral on Christmas and lay them before

the Holy Mother and Child. People saved all
through the year that they might have something
wonderful to bring on that day; and there was a
saying among them that when a gift was brought
that pleased the Christ-child more than any other
He would reach down from Mary's arms and take
it. This was but a saying, of course. The old Herr

115

Graff, the oldest man in the city, could not remember that it had ever really happened; and many there were who laughed at the very idea. But children often talked about it, and the poets made beautiful verses about it; and often when a rich gift was placed beside the altar the watchers would whisper among themselves, 'Perhaps now we shall see the miracle.'

Those who had no gifts to bring went to the cathedral just the same on Christmas Eve to see the gifts of the others and hear the carols and watch the burning of the waxen tapers. The little clock-maker was one of these. Often he was stopped and someone would ask, 'How happens it that you never bring a gift?' Once the Bishop himself questioned him: 'Poorer than thou have brought offerings to the Child. Where is thy gift?'

Then it was that Hermann had answered:

'Wait; some day you shall see. I, too, shall bring a gift some day.'

The truth of it was that the little clock-maker was so busy giving away all the year that there was never anything left at Christmas-time. But he had a wonderful idea on which he was working every minute that he could spare time from his clocks. It had taken him years and years; no-one knew anything about it but Trude, his neighbour's child, and Trude had grown from a baby into a little house-mother, and still the gift was not finished.

It was to be a clock, the most wonderful and beautiful clock ever made; and every part of it had been fashioned with loving care. The case, the works, the weights, the hands, and the face, all had taken years of labour. He had spent years carving the case and hands, years perfecting the works; and now Hermann saw that with a little more haste and time he could finish it for the coming Christmas. He mended the children's toys as before, but he gave up making his regular clocks, so there were fewer to sell, and often his cupboard was empty and he went supperless to bed. But that only made him a little thinner and his face a little kinder; and meantime the gift clock became more and more beautiful. It was fashioned after a rude stable with rafters, stall, and crib. The Holy Mother knelt beside the manger in which a tiny Christ-child lay, while through the open door the hours came. Three were kings and three were shepherds and three were soldiers and three were angels; and when the hours struck, the figure knelt in adoration before the sleeping Child, while the silver chimes played the 'Magnificat'.

'Thou seest,' said the clock-maker to Trude, 'it is not just on Sundays and holidays that we should remember to worship the Krist Kindlein and bring Him gifts – but every day, every hour.'

The days went by like clouds scudding before a winter wind, and the clock was finished at last. So happy was Hermann with his work that he put the gift clock on the shelf before the little window to show the passers-by. There were crowds looking at it all day long, and many would whisper, 'Do you think this can be the gift Hermann has spoken of – his offering on Christmas Eve to the Church?'

The day before Christmas came. Hermann cleaned up his little shop, wound all his clocks, brushed his clothes, and then went over the gift clock again to be sure everything was perfect.

'It will not look meanly beside the other gifts,' he thought, happily. In fact he was so happy that he gave away all but one pfennig to the blind beggar who passed his door; and then, remembering that he had eaten nothing since breakfast, he spent that last pfennig for a Christmas apple to eat with a crust of bread he had. These he was putting by in the cupboard to eat after he was dressed, when the door opened and Trude was standing there crying softly.

118

'Kindlein – kindlein, what ails thee?' And he gathered her into his arms..

' 'Tis the father. He is hurt, and all the money that was put by for the tree and sweets and toys has gone to the Herr Doctor. And now, how can I tell the children? Already they have lighted the candle at the window and are waiting for Kriss Kringle to come.'

The clock-maker laughed merrily.

'Come, come, little one, all will be well. Hermann will sell a clock for thee. Some house in the city must need a clock; and in a wink we shall have money enough for the tree and the toys. Go home and sing.'

He buttoned on his greatcoat and, picking out the best of the old clocks, he went out. He went first to the rich merchants, but their houses were full of clocks; then to the journeymen, but they said his clock was old-fashioned. He even stood on the corners of the streets and in the square, crying, 'A clock – a good clock for sale,' but no-one paid any attention to him. At last he gathered up his courage and went to the Herr Graff himself.

'Will your Excellency buy a clock?' he said, trembling at his own boldness. 'I would not ask, but it is Christmas and I am needing to buy happiness for some children.'

119

The Herr Graff smiled.

'Yes, I will buy a clock, but not that one. I will pay a thousand gulden for the clock thou hast had in thy window these four days past.'

'But, your Excellency, that is impossible!' And poor Hermann trembled harder than ever.

'Poof! Nothing is impossible. That clock or none. Get thee home, and I will send for it in half an hour and pay thee the gulden.'

The little clock-maker stumbled out.

'Anything but that – anything but that!' he kept mumbling over and over to himself on his way home. But as he passed the neighbour's house he saw the children at the window with their lighted candle and he heard Trude singing.

And so it happened that the servant who came from the Herr Graff carried the gift clock away with him; but the clock-maker would take but five of the thousand gulden in payment. And as the servant disappeared up the street the chimes commenced to ring from the great cathedral, and the streets suddenly became noisy with the many people going thither, bearing their Christmas offerings.

'I have gone empty-handed before,' said the little clock-maker, sadly. 'I can go empty-handed once again.' And again he buttoned up his greatcoat.

As he turned to shut his cupboard door behind him his eyes fell on the Christmas apple, and an odd little smile crept into the corners of his mouth and lighted his eyes.

'It is all I have – my dinner for two days. I will carry that to the Christ-child. It is better, after all, than going empty-handed.'

How full of peace and beauty was the great cathedral when Hermann entered it! There were a thousand tapers burning and everywhere the sweet scent of the Christmas greens – and the laden altar before the Holy Mother and Child. There were richer gifts than had been brought for many years: marvellously wrought vessels from the greatest silversmiths; cloth of gold and cloth of silk brought from the East by the merchants; poets had brought their songs illuminated on rolls of heavy parchment; painters had brought their pictures of saints and the Holy Family; even the King himself had brought his crown and sceptre to lay before the Child. And after all these offerings came the little clock-maker, walking slowly down the long, dim aisle, holding tight to his Christmas apple.

The people saw him and a murmur rose,

hummed a moment indistinctly through the church and then grew clear and articulate:

'Shame! See, he is too mean to bring his clock! He hoards it as a miser hoards his gold. See what he brings! Shame!'

The words reached Hermann and he stumbled on blindly, his head dropped forward on his breast, his hands groping the way. The distance seemed interminable. Now he knew he was past the seats; now his feet touched the first step, and there were seven to climb to the altar. Would his feet never reach the top?

'One, two, three,' he counted to himself, then tripped and almost fell. 'Four, five, six.' He was nearly there. There was but one more.

The murmur of shame died away and in its place rose one of wonder and awe. Soon the words became intelligible:

'The miracle! It is the miracle!'

The people knelt in the big cathedral; the Bishop raised his hands in prayer. And the little clock-maker, stumbling to the last step, looked up through dim eyes and saw the Child leaning towards him, far down from Mary's arms, with hands outstretched to take his gift.

This story is by Ruth Sawyer.

The Lost Boy

There was one light in the village on Christmas Eve; it came from Jock Scabra's cottage, and he was the awkwardest old man that had ever lived in our village or in the island, or in the whole of Orkney.

I was feeling very wretched and very ill-natured myself that evening. My Aunty Belle had just been explaining to me after tea that Santa Claus, if he did exist, was a spirit that moved people's hearts to generosity and goodwill; no more or less.

Gone was my fat apple-cheeked red-coated friend of the past ten winters. Scattered were the reindeer, broken the sledge that had beaten such a marvellous path through the constellations and the Merry Dancers, while all the children of Orkney slept. Those merry perilous descents down the lum, Yule eve by Yule eve, with the sack of toys and books, games and chocolate boxes, had never really taken place at all . . . I looked over towards our hearth, after my aunt had finished speaking: the magic had left it, it was only a place of peat flames and peat smoke.

I can't tell you how angry I was, the more I thought about it. How deceitful, how cruel, grown-ups were! They had exiled my dear old friend, Santa Claus, to eternal oblivion. The gifts I would find in my stocking next morning would have issued from Aunty Belle's 'spirit of generosity'. It was not the same thing at all. (Most of the year I saw little enough of that spirit of generosity – at Halloween, for example, she had boxed my ears till I saw stars that had never been in the sky, for stealing a few apples and nuts out of the cupboard, before 'dooking' time.)

If there was a more ill-tempered person than my Aunty Belle in the village, it was, as I said, old Jock Scabra, the fisherman with a silver ring in his ear and a fierce one-eyed tom cat.

His house, alone in the village, was lit that

night. I saw it, from our front door, at eleven o'clock.

Aunty Belle's piece of common sense had so angered me, that I was in a state of rebellion and recklessness. No, I would *not* sleep. I would not even stay in a house from which Santa had been banished. I felt utterly betrayed and bereaved.

When, about half past ten, I heard rending snores coming from Aunty Belle's bedroom, I got out of bed stealthily and put my cold clothes on, and unlatched the front door and went outside. The whole house had betrayed me – well, I intended to be out of the treacherous house when the magic hour of midnight struck.

The road through the village was deep in snow, dark except where under old Scabra's window the lamplight had stained it an orange colour. The snow shadows were blue under his walls. The stars were like sharp nails. Even though I had wrapped my scarf twice round my neck, I shivered in the bitter night.

Where could I go? The light in the old villain's window was entrancing – I fluttered towards it like a moth. How would such a sour old creature be celebrating Christmas Eve? Thinking black thoughts, beside his embers, stroking his wicked one-eyed cat.

The snow crashed like thin fragile glass under my feet.

I stood at last outside the fisherman's window. I looked in.

What I saw was astonishing beyond ghosts or trows.

There was no crotchety old man inside, no one-eyed cat, no ingrained filth and hung cob-webs. The paraffin lamp threw a circle of soft light, and all that was gathered inside that radiance was clean and pristine: the cups and plates on the dresser, the clock and ship-in-the-bottle and tea-caddies on the mantelpiece, the framed picture of Queen Victoria on the wall, the blue stones of the floor, the wood and straw of the fireside chair, the patchwork quilt on the bed.

A boy I had never seen before was sitting at the table. He might have been about my own age, and his head was a mass of bronze ringlets. On the table in front of him were an apple, an orange, a little sailing ship crudely cut from wood, with linen sails, probably cut from an old shirt. The boy – whoever he was – considered those objects with the utmost gravity. Once he put out his finger and touched the hull of the toy ship; as if

it was so precious it had to be treated with special delicacy, lest it broke like a soap-bubble. I couldn't see the boy's face – only his bright hair, his lissom neck, and the gravity and joy that informed all his gestures. These were his meagre Christmas presents; silently he rejoiced in them.

Beyond the circle of lamp-light, were there other dwellers in the house? There may have been hidden breath in the darkened box bed in the corner.

I don't know how long I stood in the bitter night outside. My hands were trembling. I looked down at them – they were blue with cold.

Then suddenly, for a second, the boy inside the house turned his face to the window. Perhaps he had heard the tiny splinterings of snow under my boots, or my quickened heart-beats.

The face that looked at me was Jock Scabra's, but Jock Scabra's from far back at the pure source of his life, sixty winters ago, before the ring was in his ear and before bad temper and perversity had grained black lines and furrows into his face. It was as if a cloth had been taken to a tarnished web-clogged mirror.

The boy turned back, smiling, to his Christmas hoard.

I turned and went home. I lifted the latch

quietly, not to awaken Aunty Belle – or, if she knew what I had been up to that midnight, there would have been little of her 'spirit of generosity' for me. I crept, trembling, into bed.

When I woke up on Christmas morning, the 'spirit of the season' had loaded my stocking and the chair beside the bed with boxes of sweets, a Guinness Book of Records, a digital watch, a game of space wars, a cowboy hat, and a fifty pence piece. Aunty Belle stood at my bedroom door, smiling. And, 'A merry Christmas,' she said.

Breakfast over, I couldn't wait to get back to the Scabra house. The village was taken over by children with apples, snowballs, laughter as bright as bells.

I peered in at the window. All was as it had been. The piratical old man sluiced the last of his breakfast tea down his throat from a cracked saucer. He fell to picking his black-and-yellow teeth with a kipper-bone. His house was like a midden.

The one-eyed cat yawned wickedly beside the new flames in the hearth.

This story is by George Mackay Brown.

Christmas is Coming

At Christmas the wind ceased to moan. Snow lay thick on the fields and the woods cast blue shadows across it. The fir trees were like sparkling, gem-laden Christmas trees, the only ones Susan had ever seen. The orchard, with the lacy old boughs outlined with snow, was a grove of fairy trees. The woods were enchanted, exquisite, the trees were holy, and anything harmful had shrunken to a thin wisp and had retreated into the depths.

The fields lay with their unevennesses gone and paths obliterated, smooth white slopes criss-crossed by black lines running up to the woods.

More than ever the farm seemed under a spell,
like a toy in the forest, with little wooden animals
and men; a brown horse led by a stiff little
red-scarfed man to a yellow stable door; round,
white, woolly sheep clustering round a blue
trough of orange mangolds; red cows drinking
from a square, white trough, and returning to a
painted cow-house.

Footprints were everywhere on the snow,
rabbits and foxes, blackbirds, pheasants and
partridges, trails of small paws, the mark of a

brush, and the long feet of the cock pheasant and the tip-mark of his tail.

A jay flew out of the wood like a blue flashing diamond and came to the grass-plot for bread. A robin entered the house and hopped under the table while Susan sat very still and her father sprinkled crumbs on the floor.

Rats crouched outside the window, peeping out of the walls with gleaming eyes, seizing the birds' crumbs and scraps, and slowly lolloping back again.

Red squirrels ran along the walls to the back door, close to the window, to eat the crumbs on the bench where the milk cans froze. Every wild

animal felt that a truce had come with the snow, and they visited the house where there was food in plenty, and sat with paws uplifted and noses twitching.

For the granaries were full, it had been a prosperous year, and there was food for everyone. Not like the year before when there was so little hay that Mr Garland had to buy a stack in February. Three large haystacks as big as houses stood in the stackyard, thatched evenly and straight by Job Fletcher, who was the best thatcher for many a mile. Great mounds showed where the roots were buried. The brick-lined pit was filled with grains and in the barns were stores of corn.

The old brew-house was full of logs of wood, piled high against the walls, cut from trees which the wind had blown down. The coal-house with its strong ivied walls, part of the old fortress, had been stored with coal brought many a mile in the blaze of summer; twenty tons lay under the snow.

On the kitchen walls hung the sides of bacon and from hooks in the ceiling dangled great hams and shoulders. Bunches of onions were twisted in the pantry and barn, and an empty cow-house was stored with potatoes for immediate use.

The floor of the apple chamber was covered with apples, rosy apples, little yellow ones, like cowslip balls, wizenedy apples with withered, wrinkled cheeks, fat, well-fed smooth-faced apples, and immense green cookers, pointed like a house, which would burst in the oven and pour out a thick cream of the very essence of apples.

Even the cheese chamber had its cheeses this year, for there had been too much milk for the milkman, and the cheese presses had been put into use again. Some of them were Christmas cheese, with layers of sage running through the middles like green ribbons.

Stone jars like those in which the forty thieves hid stood on the pantry floor, filled with white lard, and balls of fat tied up in bladders hung from the hooks. Along the broad shelves round the walls were pots of jam, blackberry and apple, from the woods and orchard, Victoria plum from the trees on house and barn, black currant from the garden, and red currant jelly, damson cheese from the half-wild ancient trees which grew everywhere, leaning over walls, dropping their blue fruit on paths and walls, in pigsty and orchard, in field and water trough, so that Susan thought they were wild as hips and haws.

Pickles and spices filled old brown pots

decorated with crosses and flowers, like the pitchers and crocks of Will Shakespeare's time.

In the little dark wine chamber under the stairs were bottles of elderberry wine, purple, thick, and sweet, and golden cowslip wine, and hot ginger, some of them many years old, waiting for the winter festivities.

There were dishes piled with mince-pies on the shelves of the larder, and a row of plum puddings with their white calico caps, and strings of sausages, and round pats of butter, with swans and cows and wheat-ears printed upon them.

Everyone who called at the farm had to eat and drink at Christmas-tide.

A few days before Christmas Mr Garland and Dan took a bill-hook and knife and went into the woods to cut branches of scarlet-berried holly. They tied them together with ropes and dragged them down over the fields to the barn. Mr Garland cut a bough of mistletoe from the ancient hollow hawthorn which leaned over the wall by the orchard, and thick clumps of dark-berried ivy from the walls.

Indoors, Mrs Garland and Susan and Becky polished and rubbed and cleaned the furniture and brasses, so that everything glowed and glittered. They decorated every room, from the kitchen where every lustre jug had its sprig in its mouth, every brass candlestick had its chaplet, every copper saucepan and preserving-pan had its wreath of shining berries and leaves, through the hall, which was a bower of green, to the two parlours which were festooned and hung with holly and boughs of fir, and ivy berries dipped in red raddle, left over from sheep marking.

Holly decked every picture and ornament. Sprays hung over the bacon and twisted round the hams and herb bunches. The clock carried a crown on his head, and every dish-cover had a little sprig. Susan kept an eye on the lonely forgotten humble things, the jelly moulds and colanders and nutmeg-graters, and made them happy with glossy leaves. Everything seemed to speak, to ask for its morsel of greenery, and she tried to leave out nothing.

On Christmas Eve fires blazed in the kitchen and parlour and even in the bedrooms. Becky ran from room to room with the red-hot salamander which she stuck between the bars to make a blaze, and Mrs Garland took the copper warming-pan filled with glowing cinders from the kitchen fire and rubbed it between the sheets of all the beds. Susan had come down to her cosy tiny room with thick curtains at the window, and a fire in the big fireplace. Flames roared up the chimneys as Dan carried in the logs and Becky piled them on the blaze. The wind came back and tried to get in, howling at the key-holes, but all the shutters were cottered and the doors shut. The horses and mares stood in the stables, warm and happy, with nodding heads. The cows slept in the cow-houses, the sheep in the open sheds. Only Rover stood at the door of his kennel, staring up at the sky, howling to the dog in the moon, and then he, too, turned and lay down in his straw.

In the middle of the kitchen ceiling there hung the kissing-bunch, the best and brightest pieces of holly made in the shape of a large ball which dangled from the hook. Silver and gilt drops, crimson bells, blue glass trumpets, bright oranges and red polished apples, peeped and glittered through the glossy leaves. Little flags of all nations, but chiefly Turkish for some unknown reason, stuck out like quills on a hedgehog. The lamp hung near, and every little berry, every leaf, every pretty ball and apple had a tiny yellow flame reflected in its heart.

Twisted candles hung down, yellow, red, and blue, unlighted but gay, and on either side was a string of paper lanterns.

Mrs Garland climbed on a stool and nailed on

the wall the Christmas texts, 'God bless our Home', 'God is Love', 'Peace be on this House', 'A Happy Christmas and a Bright New Year'.

So the preparations were made. Susan hung up her stocking at the foot of the bed and fell asleep. But soon singing roused her and she sat, bewildered. Yes, it was the carol-singers.

Outside under the stars she could see the group of men and women, with lanterns throwing beams across the paths and on to the stable door. One man stood apart beating time, another played a fiddle and another had a flute. The rest sang in four parts the Christmas hymns, '*While Shepherds Watched*', '*O Come, all Ye faithful*', and '*Hark the Herald Angels Sing*'.

There was the Star, Susan could see it twinkling and bright in the dark boughs with their white frosted layers; and there was the stable. In a few hours it would be Christmas Day, the best day of all the year.

This story is by Alison Uttley.

The Christmas Truce

It was Hubert's mother's idea that the Outlaws versus Hubert Laneites feud should be abolished.

'Christmas, you know,' she said vaguely to William's mother, 'the season of peace and good-will. If they don't bury the hatchet at this season they never will. It's so absurd for them to go on like this. Think how much *happier* they'd be if they were *friends*.'

Mrs Brown thought, murmured, 'Er – yes,' uncertainly, and added, 'I've *tried*, you know, but boys are so funny.'

'Yes,' said Mrs Lane earnestly (Mrs Lane was large and breathless and earnest and overdressed),

143

'but they're *very* sweet, aren't they? Hubie's *awfully* sweet. I simply can't think how anyone could quarrel with Hubie. We'll make a *real* effort this Christmas to put an end to this foolish quarrel, won't we? I feel that if only your Willie got to know my Hubie properly, he'd simply love him, he would really. *Everyone* who really knows Hubie loves him.'

Mrs Brown said, 'Er – yes,' still more uncertainly, and Mrs Lane continued: 'I've thought out how to do it. If you'll invite Hubie to Willie's party, we'll *insist* on his coming, and we'll invite Willie to Hubie's, and you *insist* on his coming, and then it will be all right. They'll have got to know each other, and, I'm sure, learnt to love each other.'

Mrs Brown said, 'Er – yes,' more uncertainly than ever. She felt that Mrs Lane was being unduly optimistic, but still it *would* be nice to see the end of the feud that was always leading William into such wild and desperate adventures.

'Then we'll begin by—'

'Begin and end, my dear Mrs Brown,' said Mrs Lane earnestly, 'by making them attend each other's Christmas parties. I'm absolutely convinced that they'll *love* each other after that. I know anyway that Willie will love Hubie, because, when you really get to know Hubie, he's the most *lovable* boy you can possibly imagine.'

Mrs Brown said, 'Er – yes,' again, because she couldn't think of anything else to say, and so the matter was settled.

When it was broached to William, he was speechless with horror.

'*Him?*' he exploded fiercely when at last the power of speech returned to him. 'Ask *him* to my Christmas party? I'd sooner not have a Christmas party at all than ask *him* to it. *Him!* Why I wun't go to the *King's* Christmas party, if *he* was going to be there. Not if I had to be beheaded for it. *Him?* Well, then I jolly well won't have a party at all.'

But Mrs Brown was unexpectedly firm. The overtures, she said, had come from Hubert's mother, and they could not with decency be rejected. It was the season of peace and goodwill ('No-one's ever peaceful or goodwillin' to me at it,' put in William bitterly); and we must all bury the hatchet and start afresh.

'I don't want to bury no hatchet,' said William tempestuously, ' 'cept in his head. *Him!* Wantin' to come to my party! Cheek!'

But William's tempestuous fury was as usual of no avail against his mothers' gentle firmness.

'It's no use, William,' she said. 'I've *promised*. He's to come to your party, and you're to go to his, and Mrs Lane is quite sure that you'll be real friends after it.'

'*Me* friends with *him*!' exploded William. 'I'll never be friends with him 'cept in a lunatic asylum an'—'

'But William,' said his mother, stemming his flood of frenzied oratory, 'I'm sure he's a very nice little boy when you get to know him.'

William replied to this by a (partially) dumb and very realistic show of physical nausea.

But faced by the alternative of Hubert Lane and his friends as guests at his party or no party at all, William bowed to the inevitable.

'All right,' he said, 'I'll have him then an' – all right, I won't *do* anythin' to him or to any of them. I'll wait till it's all over. I'll wait till he's been to my party an' I've been to his, an' then – well, you'll be jolly sorry you ever made us do it 'cause we'll have such a lot to make up.'

Mrs Brown, however, was content with her immediate victory. She sent an invitation to Hubert Lane and to Bertie Franks (Hubert's friend and lieutenant) and to Hubert's other friends, and they all accepted in their best copper-plate handwriting. William and his Outlaws went about sunk deep in gloom.

'If it wasn't for the trifle an' the crackers,' said William darkly, 'I wouldn't have had it at all – not with *him*. An' it'll have to be a jolly fine trifle, practic'ly *all* cream, to make it worth while.' His mood grew darker and darker as the day approached. He even discussed with his Outlaws the possibility of making a raid on the larder before the party, and carrying off trifles and jellies and fruit salad into the woods, leaving the Hubert Laneites to arrive and find the cupboard bare and their hosts flown. It was a tempting plan, but after dallying with it fondly for a few days they reluctantly gave it up, as being not really worth its inevitable consequences. Instead, they steeled themselves to go through the affair in the dogged spirit of martyrdom, their sufferings allayed only by the thought of the trifle and crackers, and the riot of hostilities that could take place as soon as the enforced Christmas truce was over. For the prospect of the end of the feud brought no glow of joy to the Outlaws' hearts. Without the Hubert Lane feud life would be dull indeed.

As the day of the party drew nearer, curiosity lightened the gloom of their spirits. How would the Hubert Laneites behave? Would they come reluctantly, surlily, at the bidding of authority, or would they come in a Christmas spirit of peace and goodwill, genuinely anxious to bury the hatchet? The later possibility was too horrible to contemplate. Rather let them come in the spirit in which the Outlaws were prepared to receive them – a spirit in which one receives a deadly foe in time of truce, all their thoughts and energies centred on the happy moment when hostilities might be resumed.

William, of course, could not watch the preparations for his party and maintain unbroken his pose of aloof displeasure. The trifle was, he was convinced, the finest trifle that had yet been seen in the neighbourhood; there were jellies of every shape and hue, there was a cream blancmange decorated with cherries and angelica, and there was an enormous iced Christmas cake. *And* there were crackers. In the eyes of William and his friends it was the crackers that lent the final touch of festivity to the tea.

The Outlaws and their supporters, as arranged, arrived first, and stood round William like a body-guard awaiting the arrival of the Hubert Laneites. They wore perfectly blank expressions, prepared to meet the Hubert Laneites in whatever guise they presented themselves. And the guise in which they ultimately presented themselves was worse than the Outlaws' worst fears. They were not surly foes, forced reluctantly to simulate neutrality, nor were they heralds of peace and goodwill. They advanced upon their host with an oily friendliness that was nauseating. They winked at each other openly. They said, 'Thanks *so* much for asking us, William. It was ripping of you. Oh, I say . . . what *topping* decorations!'

And they nudged each other and sniggered. William clenched his fists in his coat pocket and did swift mental calculations. His party would be over in four hours. In four days' time Hubert's party would come, and that would last about four hours, and then, *then*, THEN they could jolly well look out for themselves. The right hand that was clenched tightly in his coat for safety's sake was itching to plant itself firmly in Hubert's smug and smiling face. Mrs Brown, of course, was deceived by their show of friendliness.

'There, William,' she whispered triumphantly, 'I knew it would be all right. They're so nice really, and *so* grateful to you for asking them. I'm sure you'll be the *greatest* friends after this. His mother *said* that he was a nice little boy.'

William did not reply to this because there wasn't anything that he could trust himself to say. He was still restraining himself with great difficulty from hurling himself upon his foes. They went in to tea.

'Oh, I say how *ripping*! How *topping*!' said the Hubert Laneites gushingly to Mrs Brown, nudging each other and sniggering whenever her eye was turned away from them. Once Hubert looked at William and made his most challenging grimace, turning immediately to Mrs Brown to say with an ingratiating smile:

'It's a simply topping party, Mrs Brown, and it's awfully nice of you to ask us.'

Mrs Brown beamed at him and said:

'It's so nice to *have* you, Hubert,' and the other Hubert Laneites sniggered, and William kept his hands in his pockets with such violence that one of them went right through the lining. But the crowning catastrophe happened when they pulled the crackers.

Hubert went up to William, and said, 'See what I've got out of a cracker, William,' and held up a ring that sent a squirt of water into William's face. The Hubert Laneites went into paroxysms of silent laughter. Hubert was all smirking contrition.

'I say, I'm so sorry, William, I'd no idea that it would do that. I'm frightfully sorry, Mrs Brown.

I'd no idea that it would do that. I just got it out
of one of the crackers. I say, I'm *so* sorry,
William.'

It was evident to everyone but Mrs Brown that
the ring had not come out of a cracker, but had
been carefully brought by Hubert in order to play
this trick on William. William was wiping water
out of his eyes and ears.

'It's quite all right, dear,' said Mrs Brown. 'It
was *quite* an accident, we all saw. They shouldn't

have such nasty things in crackers, but it wasn't your fault. Tell him that you don't mind a bit, William.'

But William hastily left the room.

'Now let's go and have a few games, shall we?' said Mrs Brown.

Ginger followed William upstairs, and found him on the hearthrug in his bedroom, kneeling over a bolster that he was violently pummelling. Ginger knew that to William the bolster was not the bolster, but Hubert Lane's plump, well-nourished body. William raised a shining purple face from his task, and then the glow faded from it as he realized that the prostrate form before him was merely the bolster, and that Hubert Lane was triumphantly sniggering among his friends downstairs, not yet overtaken by Nemesis.

'Why don't you go down and smash his face in?' said Ginger simply.

William, returning reluctantly to Reality, raised the limp form of the bolster, and threw it on to the bed.

'Can't,' he said tersely, 'can't do anything not while he's in our house. I—'

'William, darling,' called his mother, 'come down, we're going to begin the games.'

William and Ginger went downstairs, and the

rest of the party passed off uneventfully. The Hubert Laneites said goodbye at the end with nauseous gratitude, and went sniggering down the drive.

'*There*, William!' said Mrs Brown, as she shut the door, 'I knew it would be all right. They were so grateful and they enjoyed it *so* much and you're *quite* friends now, aren't you?'

But William was already upstairs in his bedroom, pummelling his bolster with such energy that he burst his collar open. During the days that intervened between William's party and Hubert Lane's party, the Hubert Laneites kept carefully out of the way of the Outlaws. Yet the Outlaws felt uneasily that something was brewing. Not content with scoring over them at William's party, Hubert meant to score over them in some way at his own. The Hubert Laneites looked upon the truce, not as something that tied their hands for the time being, but as something that delivered their enemies into their power. William was uneasily aware that Hubert Lane would not feel the compunction that he had felt in the matter of his guests.

'We've gotter do somethin' to them at their party, same as they did to us at ours,' said Ginger firmly.

'Yes, but what can we do?' said William. 'We can't start fightin' 'em. We've promised not to. An' – an' there's nothin' else we *can* do. Jus' wait, jus' *wait* till their party's over.'

And William's fists curled themselves zestfully as he danced his most fiendish war dance in the middle of the road (his bolster had been so badly used lately that nearly all the feathers were coming out. Mrs Brown had asked him only that morning what on earth he was doing to it).

'But they'll never forget that water squirt,' said Ginger mournfully.

'Unless we do somethin' back,' said Douglas.

'What *can* we do in *their* house with them watchin' us all the time?' said Henry.

'We mus' jus' *think*,' said William, 'there's four days an' we'll think hard.'

But the day of Hubert's party arrived, and they'd thought of nothing. William looked downcast and spiritless. Even pummelling his bolster had lost its charm for him.

They met in the old barn in the morning to arrange their plan of action, but none of them could think of any plan of action to arrange, and the meeting broke up gloomily at lunch-time, without having come to any decision at all.

William walked slowly and draggingly through

the village on his way home. His mother had told him to stop at the baker's with an order for her, and it was a sign of his intense depression that he remembered to do it. In ordinary circumstances William forgot his mother's messages in the village. He entered the baker's shop, and stared around him resentfully. It seemed to be full of people. He'd have to wait all night before anyone took any notice of him. Just his luck, he reflected bitterly . . . Then he suddenly realized that the mountainous lady just in front of him was Mrs Lane. She was talking in a loud voice to a friend.

'Yes, Hubie's party is this afternoon. We're having William Brown and his friends. To put a stop to that silly quarrel that's gone on so long, you know. Hubie's so lovable that I simply can't think how anyone could quarrel with him. But, of course, it will be all right after today. We're having a Father Christmas, you know. Bates, our gardener, is going to be the Father Christmas and give out presents. I've given Hubie three pounds to get some *really* nice presents for it to celebrate the ending of the feud.'

William waited his turn, gave his message, and went home for lunch.

★   ★   ★

Immediately after lunch he made his way to Bates's cottage.

It stood on the road at the end of the Lanes' garden. One gate led from the garden to the road, and the other from the garden to the Lanes' shrubbery. Behind the cottage was Bates's treasured kitchen garden, and at the bottom was a little shed where he stored his apples. The window of the shed had to be open for airing purposes, but Bates kept a sharp look out for his perpetual and inveterate enemies, boys.

William approached the cottage with great circumspection, looking anxiously around to be sure that none of the Hubert Laneites was in sight. He had reckoned on the likelihood of their all being engaged in preparation for the party.

He opened the gate, walked up the path, and knocked at the door, standing poised on one foot ready to turn to flee should Bates, recognizing him and remembering some of his former exploits in his kitchen garden, attack him on sight. He heaved a sigh of relief, however, when Bates opened the door. It was clear that Bates did not recognize him. He received him with an ungracious scowl, but that, William could see, was because he was *a* boy, not because he was *the* boy.

'Well?' said Bates sharply, holding the door open a few inches, 'what d'you want?'

William assumed an ingratiating smile, the smile of a boy who has every right to demand admittance to the cottage.

'I say,' he said with a fairly good imitation of the Hubert Laneites' most patronizing manner, 'you've got the Father Christmas things here, haven't you?'

The ungraciousness of Bates's scowl did not relax, but he opened the door a few inches wider in a resigned fashion. He had been pestered to death over the Father Christmas things. These boys had been in and out of his cottage all day with parcels and what not, trampling over his doorstep and 'mussing up' everything. He'd decided some time ago that it wasn't going to be worth the five shillings that Mrs Lane was giving him for it. He took for granted that William was one of the Hubert Laneites coming once more to 'muss up' his bag of parcels, and take one out or put one in, or snigger over them as they'd been doing every day for the last week. But he *did* think that they'd have left him in peace on the very afternoon of the party.

'Yes,' he said surlily, 'I've got the things, 'ere an' they're all right, so there's no call to start upsettin' of 'em again. I've had enough of you comin' in an' mussin' the place up.'

'I only wanted to count them, and make sure that we've got the right number,' said William with an oily friendliness that was worthy of Hubert himself.

The man opened the door with a shrug.

'All right,' he said, 'go in and count 'em. I tell you, I'm sick of the whole lot of you, I am. Mussin' the place up. Look at your boots!'

William looked at his boots, made an ineffectual attempt to wipe them on the mat, and entered the cottage. He had an exhilarating sense of danger and adventure as he entered. At any minute he might arouse the man's suspicions. His ignorance of where the presents were, for instance, when he was supposed to have been visiting them regularly, might give him away completely. Moreover, a Hubert Laneite might arrive any minute and trap him, in the cottage. It was, in short, a situation after William's own heart. The immediate danger of discovery was averted by Bates himself, who waved him irascibly into the back parlour, where the presents were evidently kept. William entered, and threw a quick glance out of the window. Yes, Ginger was there, as they had arranged he should be, hovering near the shed where the apples were sorted. Then he looked round the room. A red cloak and hood and white beard were spread out on the sofa, and on the hearthrug lay a sackful of small parcels.

'Well, count 'em for goodness' sake an' let's get a bit of peace,' said Bates more irritably than ever. William fell on his knees and began to make a pretence of counting the parcels. Suddenly he looked up and gazed out of the window.

'I say!' he said, 'there's a boy taking your apples.'

Bates leapt to the window. There, upon the roof of the shed, was Ginger, with an arm through the open window, obviously in the act of purloining apples and carefully exposing himself to view.

With a yell of fury Bates sprang to the door and down the path towards the shed. He had forgotten everything but this outrage upon his property. Left alone, William turned his attention quickly to the sack. It contained parcels, each one labelled and named. He had to act quickly. Bates had set off after Ginger, but he might return at any minute. Ginger's instructions were to lure him on by keeping just out of reach, but Bates might tire of the chase before they'd gone a few yards, and, remembering his visitor, return to the cottage in order to prevent his 'mussin'' things up any more than necessary. William had no time to investigate. He had to act solely upon his suspicions and his knowledge of the characters of Hubert and his friends. Quickly he began to change the labels of the little parcels, putting the one marked William on to the one marked Hubert, and exchanging the labels of the Outlaws and their supporters for those of the Hubert Laneites and their supporters. Just as he was fastening the last one, Bates returned, hot and breathless.

'Did you catch him?' said William, secure in the knowledge that Ginger had outstripped Bates more times than any of them could remember.

'Naw,' said Mr Bates, panting and furious. 'I'd like to wring his neck. I'd larn him if I got hold of him. Who was he? Did you see?'

'He was about the same size as me,' said William in the bright, eager tone of one who is trying to help, 'or he may have been just a *tiny* bit smaller.'

Bates turned upon him, as if glad of the chance to vent his irascibility upon somebody.

'Well, you clear out,' he said, 'I've had enough of you mussin' the place up, an' you can tell the others that they can keep away too. An' I'll be glad when it's over, I tell you. I'm sick of the lot of you.'

Smiling the patronizing smile that he associated with the Hubert Laneites, William took a hurried departure, and ran home as quickly as he could. He found his mother searching for him despairingly.

'Oh, William, where *have* you been? You ought to have begun to get ready for the party *hours* ago.'

I've just been for a little walk,' said William casually. 'I'll be ready in time all right.'

With the unwelcome aid of his mother, he was ready in time, spick and span and spruce and shining.

'I'm so *glad* that you're friends now and that that silly quarrel's over,' said Mrs Brown as she saw him off. 'You feel much *happier* now that you're friends, don't you?'

William snorted sardonically, and set off down the road.

The Hubert Laneites received the Outlaws with even more nauseous friendliness than they had shown at William's house. It was evident, however, from the way they sniggered and nudged each other that they had some plan prepared. William felt anxious. Suppose that the plot they had so obviously prepared had nothing to do with the Father Christmas . . . Suppose that he had wasted his time and trouble that morning . . . They went into the hall after tea, and Mrs Lane said roguishly:

'Now, boys, I've got a visitor for you.' Immediately Bates, inadequately disguised as Father Christmas and looking fiercely resentful of the whole proceedings, entered with his sack. The Hubert Laneites sniggered delightedly. This was evidently the crowning moment of the afternoon. Bates took the parcels out one by one, announcing the name on each label.

The first was William.

The Hubert Laneites watched him go up to receive it in paroxysms of silent mirth. William took it and open it, wearing a sphinx-like expression. It was the most magnificent mouth organ that he had ever seen. The mouths of the Hubert Laneites dropped open in horror and amazement. It was evidently the present that Hubert had destined for himself. Bates called out Hubert's name. Hubert, his mouth still hanging open with horror and amazement, went to receive his parcel. It contained a short pencil with shield and rubber of the sort that can be purchased for a penny or twopence. He went back to his seat blinking. He examined his label. It bore his name. He examined William's label. It bore his name. There was no mistake about it. William was thanking Mrs Lane effusively for his present.

'Yes, dear,' she was saying, 'I'm so glad you like it. I haven't had time to look at them but I told Hubie to get nice things.'

Hubert opened his mouth to protest, and then shut it again. He was beaten and he knew it. He couldn't very well tell his mother that he'd spent the bulk of the money on the presents for himself and his particular friends, and had spent only a few coppers on the Outlaws' presents. He couldn't think what had happened. He'd been so sure that it would be all right. The Outlaws would hardly have had the nerve publicly to object to their presents, and Mrs Lane was well meaning but conveniently short sighted, and took for granted that everything that Hubie did was perfect. Hubert sat staring at his pencil and blinking his eyes in incredulous horror. Meanwhile the presentation was going on. Bertie Franks' present was a ruler that could not have cost more than a penny, and Ginger's was a magnificent electric torch. Bertie stared at the torch with an expression that would have done credit to a tragic mask, and Ginger hastened to establish his permanent right to his prize by going up to thank Mrs Lane for it.

'Yes, it's lovely, dear,' she said, 'I told Hubie to get nice things.'

Douglas's present was a splendid penknife, and Henry's a fountain-pen, while the corresponding presents for the Hubert Laneites were an india-rubber and a note-book. The Hubert Laneites watched their presents passing into the enemies' hands with expressions of helpless agony. But Douglas's parcel had more than a penknife in it. It had a little bunch of imitation flowers with an india-rubber bulb attached and a tiny label, 'Show this to William and press the rubber thing.' Douglas took it to Hubert. Hubert knew it, of course, for he had bought it, but he was paralysed with horror at the whole situation.

'Look, Hubert,' said Douglas.

A fountain of ink caught Hubert neatly in the eye. Douglas was all surprise and contrition.

'I'm so sorry, Hubert,' he said, 'I'd no idea that it was going to do that. I've just got it out of my parcel and I'd no idea that it was going to do that. I'm so sorry, Mrs Lane. I'd no idea that it was going to do that.'

'Of course you hadn't, dear,' said Mrs Lane. 'It's Hubie's own fault for buying a thing like that. It's very foolish of him indeed.'

Hubert wiped the ink out of his eyes and sputtered helplessly.

Then William discovered that it was time to go.

'Thank you so much for our lovely presents, Hubert,' he said politely, 'we've had a *lovely* time.'

And Hubert, under his mother's eye, smiled a green and sickly smile.

The Outlaws marched triumphantly down the

road, brandishing their spoils. William was playing on his mouth organ, Ginger was flashing his
electric light, Henry waving his fountain-pen, and
Douglas slashing at the hedge with his penknife.

Occasionally they turned round to see if their
enemies were pursuing them, in order to retrieve
their treasures.

But the Hubert Laneites were too broken in
spirit to enter into open hostilities just then.

As they walked, the Outlaws raised a wild and
inharmonious paean of triumph.

And over the telephone Mrs Lane was saying
to Mrs Brown:

'Yes, dear, it's been a complete success. They're
the *greatest* friends now. I'm sure it's been a
Christmas that they'll all remember all their lives.'